Rosemary shivered and pulled her sweater closer. Could whatever took her bike, the hibachi, Mom's clothes, and Dad's teacup be something from the past?

"Remember," Dad said, standing up, "'We cannot escape history,' as old Abe used to say."

Blasts of air shook the old windows, and they rattled in their frames. The rug puffed in one corner and something wailed outside.

Slowly, Rosemary got up and went through the cold study to the kitchen. The fluorescent light over the sink made the kitchen look like a moonscape. It was completely black outside.

"Open the door, Rosie!" Dad's voice came from the living room.

She jumped at a touch on her shoulder. Nicky stood behind her.

"It's a little spooky out there, isn't it," he said comfortably, opening the door. The night blew around them. Trees rattled and shook, and the wind and rain ricocheted around the house. Something squealed nearby and Rosemary slammed the door.

"What is it, Nicky? Oh, what *is* it?"

It came again, a high-pitched squealing, and Nicky stepped closer to the door. "Don't know, I can't see."

"Don't—let—it—be—anything—scary—or—hurting."

ANN TURNER

Rosemary's Witch

A Charlotte Zolotow Book

HarperTrophy
A Division of HarperCollinsPublishers

Library of Congress Cataloging-in-Publication Data
Turner, Ann Warren.
    Rosemary's witch / by Ann Turner.
        p.   cm.
    "A Charlotte Zolotow book."
    Summary: After moving into an old house in a small New England
town, nine-year-old Rosemary discovers that the nearby woods conceal a
150-year-old witch, who once lived in the house and is using her magic
to take it back.
    ISBN 0-06-026127-7. — ISBN 0-06-026128-5 (lib. bdg.)
    ISBN 0-06-440494-3 (pbk.)
    [1. Witches—Fiction.   2. Fantasy.]   I. Title.
PZ7.T8535Ro   1991   90-39779
[Fic]—dc20   CIP
                                                                 AC

First Harper Trophy edition, 1994.

For my two brothers: Nicholas, who is still beautiful, and Peter (model for Ernie) who is still cozy

Contents

Rosemary's
Witch

Chapter 1

In the smoky blue-green hills of summer, where the phoebe calls and hawks sail lazily overhead, is a town called Woodhaven. That is where it began.

It was a town like a hat someone had thrown away for being too plain, for not having bird wings on it or bobbing strawberries. It had one street that ran straight through town. There was a post office; Bob's Soda Shop, which sold shoelaces and fish hooks in February, Easter eggs and hunting mittens in July; one restaurant run by Mrs. Nan and all her regulars; a grange hall where square dances were held; a church with a gold-topped steeple; one brick schoolhouse; and a library. That was small and cool because it was built of stone. It smelled of moss and stream water. Behind the library was a river that rushed under a cement bridge. You could fish from it and catch trout no bigger than your hand. If you showed your fish to Mrs. Nan, she'd yell, "Hey! If I wanted to buy *tripe*, I'd buy it at the store, honey!" For the old houses by the river still put sewage into the water.

Into this dreaming, sleepy town came a collection of new people—though one was not exactly a person and not exactly new—whose lives were to be knitted together.

Number 1—Mr. Morgenthau. "Morgenthau?" he said to his mother long ago. "Why not Gray or Smith?" His mother smiled, patted his hair, and now George was used to his name. He often said, "That's what getting older is—getting used to things." Mr. Morgenthau was tall and softly rounded with a long, kind face, large ears, and thinning hair. He was the new professor of history at the local college. Mr. Morgenthau wanted a house of his own—a big, gracious house with wide floorboards, rooms that let the breeze flow through, and bookcases for his Abraham Lincoln collection.

Two—Mrs. Morgenthau. She was small and lean with red curly hair. She stood on the tips of her toes like a racer at the starting line and was the new dance teacher at the same local college. "Turn, pirouette, *work* those legs, up, down, up, down!" She wanted a home of her own with a room to dance in and a place where her children could gather memories—Queen Anne's lace in the meadow, fireflies in late June, snowmen in winter.

4

Three—Nicholas, their eleven-year-old son. He had black hair, green eyes, and a collection of rocks with markings on them: a bird's feather, an insect's wing. He liked the idea of a rock holding pieces of time. When he held that rock, he felt he touched time—dinosaur tracks, steamy giant ferns, the cries of long-ago birds. Nicholas wanted a house with a barn and a field to dig for arrowheads in.

Four—Rosemary, his sister, aged nine. She had a shock of straight brown hair and a body that was full of angles and sharp corners. Rosemary made them stop the car when they passed an oily rag. "Stop, it's a wounded blue jay!" Nicholas would snap, "No, it's just a rag, silly!" She collected wounded creatures: a bald gerbil that limped, a chipmunk with three legs, four orphaned baby mice, and something brown that fell from a tree. She wanted an old house with a room of her own, rose wallpaper, and a window over-looking a field.

Their desire for a home was so deep they could almost taste it, as if you woke late in the night with the rich aroma of chocolate on your tongue. And when they finally found the house they were looking for, tucked away in Woodhaven on top of a hill, they could hardly believe it was theirs.

"What I don't understand," Johnny Preston said after it was all over, "what I don't understand is why all that stuff happened this past summer. Why then?"

Mrs. Nan pushed back her flyaway hair and plunked her

elbows on the counter. "Well, remember what I told you my great-aunt Emily said about the town?"

"Yeah, I remember," Johnny sipped his coffee and swallowed. One of the regulars coughed beside him.

"I wonder," Neil Baldwin started. "I wonder if that family buying that house had something to do with it."

"The Morgenthaus?" Mrs. Nan grimaced. "No, why should it? That was just a coincidence."

"Well, they did come at the same time all that bad stuff started to happen," Phil, another regular, said. "And they were kind of different, if you know what I mean."

"Yeah," said Mrs. Nan. "Dancers and history professors. But nice," she hastened to add.

Johnny set down his coffee cup, stood, and straightened his hat. "I don't believe in coincidence. I think it was time."

"What d'ya mean, *time*?" asked Mrs. Nan, almost glaring at him.

"Just time," said Johnny, slamming the door. And the regulars nodded and sighed, "It was time, yup, time."

Mathilda Arrives

She found the cottage one day as she flew low over her woods. Mathilda almost missed it, the black, rotting roof hidden by two pines. She settled slowly to the earth and walked in.

A tin cup rolled in the corner near a pile of wet leaves. Broken boards littered the floor, and the glass was cracked in the one window.

"Home." The word squeezed out. The edges of her mouth flaked. "Home," she creaked. Not a cave. Not a dark, wet hole in a rock. She sighed. What was it that a home needed? With one part of her unfolded brain, Mathilda remembered. She'd had a home once. With windows and curtains and a cat.

Her chest ached, and Mathilda rubbed it, moaning. "Things." She needed things to sleep on, eat on. As the woods darkened outside, she passed through the door and rose rapidly into the air. She flew straight to the Salvation Army box in town and reached inside. One brown overcoat with brass buttons; one mustard-colored turtleneck; canvas sneakers with purple heart laces; a bandana the color of rotten plums. Mathilda plunged into the clothes, and they settled around her.

She swooped down on a red garage near her woods, grabbed some plywood, a sheet of blue plastic, a blanket, an embroidered pillow saying "Mother," and a trash bag full of bits and pieces. That was where the fat boy lived with his mother and a dog. She'd known a boy like him once long ago. He'd hurt her. Then on to the next house with its old white shed she knew so well. It was empty, but not for long, she knew. When they came, she would take it all back.

She racheted home in the wind and dropped through the open roof. In one corner she set up the plywood with a folded blanket on top and put the embroidered pillow saying "Mother" against the wall. Mother. What was a mother? Dimly she remembered somebody small and slim who sometimes sang in the mornings. Long ago. Who once brought her something hot in a cup when she was sick in bed.

Mathilda went to the corner and picked up the battered

8

tin cup. She sucked stream water through the open door into the cup, stuffed dried moss in, and hissed.

"Ah. Tea." The words jerked out, strange in her mouth. She tossed an old rag rug on the floor and propped her naked, yellowing feet on it.

The wind shook the cabin and a sudden gust blasted through, upsetting Mathilda's cup of dried-moss tea. She shot straight through the roof with the plastic in her teeth and hammered it down against the creaking roof with her own gnarled fist. The nails were twigs she drove straight through.

Mathilda settled slowly to the couch, pursed her lips, and sucked the cooling tea off the floor.

The wind shook branches outside and something fell to the ground. A rotten branch. "Rotten." That's what *they* had called her all those years ago as they danced around her in the playground. High, shrill voices rising out of cruel, red mouths. "Rotten." They would pay. Even if those children were all dead now, their great-grandchildren were alive. They were no different, and they would suffer the way she had suffered.

Mathilda sat on the couch and massaged her gums. They hurt. She wasn't sure if her teeth were falling out and something else was coming in, or if her teeth were getting longer, larger, yellower. She jumped up and peered in the cabin window. Just the same. Ageless, pale skin, black eyes, moles like scattered fungi. She patted her hair and it sprang off to one side. "Quiet!" she shouted. The hair lay flat for a moment and then hissed behind her.

Mathilda rubbed her arms. Everything ached. It was the problem with being 149 years old, but that did not matter now that she was here where she had always meant to be. Soon it would be her 150th birthday. That was a time of power and change. She was sure she had the power now, and the only thing left was to begin.

Chapter 2

The car was hot and stuffy. It smelled of old blankets and the banana Rosemary had left in the backseat.

"How much farther?" Rosemary asked. She wanted to bounce on the seat and whine. "*When* are we getting *out* of this car?"

"Soon." Father drummed his fingers on the wheel. "Soon, Rosie."

Mother sighed. Her red curls lay flat against her scalp, and her arm drooped against the car window.

"She'd better be honest with us," Mother grumbled. "The last house Mrs. Morton showed!" She flung her hands and waved them rapidly. "Unfit for human beings!"

"That doesn't begin to describe it," Nicholas whispered to Rosemary.

"That barn," she whispered back, "full of chicken feathers."

"And chicken stink. Peeoouuw!"

"And they had those stupid plastic flowers stuck all over the front lawn—"

"Like a funeral," Nicholas finished.

Rosemary looked out the window. They were driving through a town small and ordinary, and she liked it because it was like her. They passed Bob's Soda Shop, Mrs. Nan's Restaurant, a brick schoolhouse, thumped over a cement bridge, and passed a church. Rosemary saw the clock on the steeple with its arms at three o'clock. Only it was later than that, she thought.

Father sped up a hill, past a cemetery with black slate stones, past a grove of tall pines. He turned into a drive, went up a slope, and stopped in front of a tall white house.

Mother jumped out first. "It's so cool!" She stretched her arms and legs.

Nicholas got out, sniffed the air, and closed his eyes. "An old field, full of ancient arrowheads and things to dig up." He opened his eyes and smiled at the meadow.

Rosemary ran to the front step and pressed her nose against the glass door. There was a wide kitchen with a wood-burning stove and a doorway leading to a study. Dad leaned over her.

"A study, Rosie! A place for all my books. Every history professor needs his own study!"

"Rosemary," she whispered. "My name is Rosemary." She'd decided that a new place deserved a new name, and she was tired of Rosie. Rosemary was full of possibility; Rosie was tired and left behind, like their last house in Garden City.

"What's that, Rosie?" Dad pressed his nose against the glass and rubbed her shoulder.

Mother joined them. "Oh, George, it's what I've always wanted." She hopped over a low railing onto the side porch. "We can watch thunderstorms from here and shooting stars. We can catch fireflies in the meadow and make up ghost stories in the dark."

"You can," Rosemary said, "not me!" Why anyone would want to be frightened was more than she could understand. As Dad might say, "There are enough scary things in this world already." She stood back and looked at the tall white house with faded green shutters. It felt like a favorite armchair in a corner waiting for someone to curl up in it. Beyond the porch a lawn ran down to the road, shaded by a huge maple. Rosemary turned. Behind her was more grass and a red barn. She saw a wild, puffed cat scoot under the barn door. Maybe she could feed it and tame it.

"Lilacs, George!" Mother pointed to the purple flowering bush beside the kitchen door.

13

Dad took a stance and proclaimed,

"When lilacs last in the dooryard bloom'd
And the great star early droop'd in the western sky in the
night . . ."

Rosemary listened to the round words spilling out of his mouth; he made words sound so easy.

He broke off. "Marjorie, this house is so old it's *leaking* history from every crack!"

Mother smiled fondly at him and turned her head. A green Cadillac nosed up the drive, crunching gravel, and stopped on the grass.

"Awful car," Dad whispered. "Now, not a word about how much we like the house!"

A doll-like woman in a frilly pink dress tottered toward them.

"Look at those shoes," Nicholas whispered. "Right out of the fifties."

"How d'you like it?" she called. "Cute, huh? Not quite 'charm on the farm,' but quaint." She seized on the word and repeated it firmly. "Quaint."

"Yes," Dad said and pointed at the roof. "Slate roof, Mrs. Morton, difficult and expensive to repair. Gutters in a sad state. Front doorstep cracked. House needs new paint. However,"—he paused and sighed,—"let's see the inside. Perhaps that will be in better shape."

Coughing nervously, the real estate woman led them into

14

the kitchen. Somewhere a crow cawed, and Rosemary, last to go in, looked back. The meadow stretched rich and green to the woods. The pines seemed like a high forbidding wall. She thought the pines swayed, though there was no wind. Suddenly Rosemary felt as if a dark cloud hung ominously above her, and she hurried inside to stand close to her mother. Mother squeezed her shoulder as Mrs. Morton chanted:

"Fine eighteenth-century room—see the original beams and the fireplace—wide pine floorboards, too."

"I'm surprised no one's bought it yet," said Mother.

"Oh, well," Mrs. Morton cut in, "most people want a small ranch, not a big house like this. Not everyone appreciates history."

Dad smiled at her and nodded as Mrs. Morton extolled more points about the house.

Nicholas signaled to Rosemary with a lift of his head, and she followed him upstairs. To the right of the landing was a sunny room with blue walls and two windows.

"Look, Rosie, this could be my room with a real bed, not a fold-out couch, and a place for my rock collection."

"Rosemary!" she said. "My name is Rosemary."

Nicky smiled. "Okay, Rose-merry."

She chased him down the hall and back, and they sat, panting, on the floor. "It's huge, Rosemary! Five bedrooms. Mom could have one just for practicing dance."

"Not like Garden City." Rosemary wrinkled her nose.

Their last house had been a squashed cube with tiny rooms and ceilings that rattled when the wind blew. Before that they'd lived in an apartment overlooking "trash park," as Nicky called it, and there was a woman upstairs who moaned on dark days.

"Do you think," Rosemary began and stopped.

"Think what?"

"Think that there's something wrong with this house?" She tasted the words on her tongue. "Wrong" felt like a sourball.

"How could anything be wrong?"

She stood and went to the window, looking out at the meadow and the wall of pines. She couldn't explain to Nicky what she felt. He'd ask her questions and ask her to be logical when she couldn't. "I don't know—just wrong. I mean, it's a huge house and no one's bought it and doesn't that seem a bit funny?"

He shook his head. "Nope. As that lady said, everyone wants ranch houses with bars in the basement."

"Oh, you!" She gave him a shove and they raced downstairs.

"Let's explore," Nicky said over his shoulder, and they ran across the back lawn to the red barn. Dust puffed over their feet, and it smelled cool and damp. Light came in patches through the windows, giving a mysterious, cavelike feel to the barn.

"Look." Nicholas took an old scythe from the wall and swung it back and forth. "We can cut the meadow with this."

"*You* can, not me! It'd take forever. Look, are those stalls?"

They went to the back of the barn, where three stalls were squeezed side by side. Rosemary ran her finger over the worn wood. "Look, teeth marks, Nicky!"

He bent over and peered at the gouges in the wood.

"Probably goats or horses, chewing on the wood. Let's go upstairs."

The stairway was dark, and the edges of the boards lifted under their feet. In the big central space were old barn beams, crisscrossing and making a house within a house. Birds' nests were ranged along one beam, nest after muddy nest. Against the wall were two rows of boxes with leftover pieces of straw.

Rosemary stuck her hand in one and pulled out a feather. "For chickens, Nicky! Look at that. We could raise chickens and have our own eggs."

"You can. Not me. They smell." He ran downstairs and she followed. Halfway down, Rosemary stopped. Her hand gripped for a railing and found the rough wall instead. The hair rose on the back of her neck.

"Oooh. What is it, Nicky?"

He turned. "What is what?"

17

"That sound." They listened quietly. Rosemary heard it again—a dry, gritty sound like sand crunching underfoot or a nail scraping against a blackboard.

"Didn't you hear it?" Rosemary felt the splintery wood of the wall. It was safe and everyday—not like that unnamed, awful sound.

"Hear what?" Nicholas picked up the scythe and swung it.

"That sound like crunching sand or someone scratching something. Maybe that's why no one bought this house." She went to the door and looked out. Everything seemed safe and calm. Green grass. Blue sky. Dark pines. Black crows spiraling and diving over the woods. She rubbed her arms.

Nicholas joined her in the doorway and said loudly, "No, I didn't hear it—must be the wind in the pines, Rosie. You've lived in the city too long."

"Don't tell me you didn't hear it. I can see the goose-bumps on your arm." She held up hers and he slowly raised his. Both arms were puckered with bumps.

It figured, Rosemary thought, that Nicholas would pretend to hear nothing. She had hunches. Nicholas had reasons. Rosemary sometimes saw things before they happened; Nicholas, always after they happened. She loved him, but sometimes it seemed he lived in another country she could not visit.

The front door of the house opened suddenly, and her

parents came out, followed by Mrs. Morton. Was she imagining it, or did that woman stop for a second and look at the woods? Then Mrs. Morton smiled, a narrow, sunless smile.

Rosemary could hear them talking. "Call the bank—speak to the owners—draw up a buy/sell agreement—"

Everyone smiled, shook hands longer than necessary, and Mrs. Morton tottered back to her Cadillac.

"Good-bye!" Mother and Father waved as the car slid down the drive and disappeared. Mother took quick running steps and leaped into the air. Ever after, Rosemary saw her mother outlined against the blue—legs outstretched, arms reaching high, and mouth open in a shout of joy. "It's ours!"

And as if something had poked her, Rosemary whispered, "No, it's not ours—not yet."

Mathilda and Emily

She found the doll one morning when she was roaming the woods. Mathilda liked the way the branches scratched her face and little flecks of blood landed on the leaves below. Like leaving a trail behind. Mathilda was here.

By the stream, where once children had played—you could see the frayed grapevines and the bark peeled off where many hands had gripped them—a foot stuck out from a rock.

Mathilda knelt and lifted the rock carefully. Underneath was a blackened cloth face with no eyes, pieces of moldy hair, and a body torn down the middle. The stuffing was almost gone, taken by mouse families for their young.

"Poor thing," Mathilda creaked, clasping it to what remained of her bosom. "What are you?" Part of her brain sparked and Mathilda jumped. Once. She had had something like this once. Mama had given it to her before she went away forever. It had golden hair and soft slippers. "A doll!" cried Mathilda.

She strode to the cabin with her find. She grabbed the lopsided tin pot and filled it with water from the stream. Then she piled twigs and sticks in a clearing, lit the fire by staring at it, and set the tin pot on top. Wisps of smoke curled up, making her cough. Fire. What did it remind her of? Mathilda rubbed her gums. Uncle's house, long ago. She hadn't meant to hurt anyone, just to get warm on that bitter winter's night. Mathilda shivered. In her memories, it was always night and always cold. But then bad things happened after that fire. Whispers. Pointing fingers. All had helped drive her away up to the high meadow at the edge of town where the water dripped and the bats found homes.

She shook herself and picked up the doll. She dipped the worn body into the water and let it bubble around its chin. She swished it back and forth, impervious to the heat. She laid the doll in the sun to dry while she collected dried moss and pine needles. Stuffing it into the arms and legs, Mathilda ran her tongue along the torn edges and they seamed together with no mark.

"Doll." Her mouth hurt. "Who left you—there?" Abandoned. Left alone. Cold winds and cold rain on the doll's face. Dogs nosing her. A cold rock her roof.

21

Mathilda imagined the same children who had once laughed and danced around her, taking this doll and flinging it beside the stream. Mathilda hissed and ran around the room, clutching the doll. Then she held it up and stared at it. The doll needed something.

Mathilda pulled off one of her heart shoelaces. She tore out the hearts and pasted on two for eyes and put three side by side for the mouth. The doll's hair was a thin reminder of what had once been. Mathilda rummaged in the trash bag and found pieces of purple yarn to stick on its head.

"There," she sighed. The doll looked back at her. Something strange rose up inside Mathilda. Something that made her want to run and hide, to ride screeching toward the nearest star and pull blackness around her. The doll stared at her with its heart eyes.

"Emily," Mathilda creaked. Emily was the only one who had not laughed at her all those years ago. Emily she would be and company she would be in the cold, dark nights.

Chapter 3

Rosemary stood in the driveway of their new house four weeks later and wondered how anyone could have so many boxes. It seemed impossible that all that *stuff* belonged to them.

The moving van was pulled up near the kitchen door, and Dad stood beside it, dressed in an old army jacket. He held a long list in one hand, and as each box was lifted down, he checked it off.

"No. 2—Dishes—Old." The box rattled ominously as the moving men charged through the kitchen door.

"Careful with Number Two!" Dad called. "That has my mother's china in it and a cup brought all the way from England."

"Mmmph," answered a squat man with powerful arms, large amounts of hair, and a tattoo saying "Marie." Rosemary watched him through the kitchen window. He rolled his eyes heavenward and jerked his head at his friend.

"Get him!" the gesture clearly said, and Rosemary squished her nose flat against the glass, hoping he'd see her and be disgusted. No one was allowed to make fun of her father.

"No. 3—Soup Spoons." Mother laughed when Dad checked it off. "We must be the only family in the entire world that has a whole box full of soup spoons."

"A very important tool, Marjorie. You can't make a good soup without a good spoon."

Dad had a thing about soups, Rosemary wanted to explain to the moving men. "Soups are comforting," Dad would shout, waving a bent spoon and stirring vigorously. "They knit up the soul. They feed the tired heart." But did a man who wore a tattoo saying "Marie" know anything about tired hearts, Rosemary wondered?

"No. 4—Rocks!" Nicholas said, and the two moving men groaned as they lifted down the wooden crate.

"My collection—be careful!" Nicholas walked beside them and made sure it was carefully deposited in his blue room upstairs.

The tattooed moving man, who they learned was called Stu, came down rubbing his arms. "Good thing I lift weights, Mrs. Morgenthau. That box! Why rocks?" He

24

stopped in the driveway and asked Nicholas.

"Why not rocks?" Nicholas smiled.

"Don't be a smart-lip!" Dad said. "Tell him. He deserves an answer. He had to carry them."

"I like them." Nicholas pulled on one ear. "There are secrets in them—different times, you know, bits of the past inside."

"Yeah, I know." Stu nodded. "Like 'Marie' here. She's a bit from the past!" He laughed and jumped into the truck.

Mother grinned and Dad looked embarrassed. "He means, Rosemary . . ."

She said, "I know what he means, Dad."

Then came the furniture, a parade of all the pieces they'd collected over the years. A yellow painted rocker that Mother said was her "nursing chair." She'd nursed both Rosemary and Nicholas in it. Rosemary didn't remember that part, but she was very fond of the chair and liked to sit in it when she was sad.

Then Dad's desk was lifted down, Stu complaining, "Them oak desks! They're like concrete."

"Careful." Dad trotted alongside. "Great things have been written on that desk. Will be written."

Then came Rosemary's canopy bed, dark wooden posts and frame, and a white crocheted top. She followed them upstairs.

"Over here, please," she said. "In this corner." As soon as they fitted the bed together, Rosemary pulled her old

25

bear, Freddy, out of his box and set him on the bed. Where she went, he went—soft and worn with patches of bare cloth and a smell that was all his own; a sleep smell, a musty-blanket smell, with a touch of milk.

She flopped beside Freddy and looked out the window. Outside was a linden tree. Dad said it would have white blossoms with a sweet smell next June. "We'll hear thousands of bees, Rosemary, a 'bee-loud glade.' " A piece of blue mountain showed through the leaves. Rosemary looked carefully; no street lights, no cars humming by, no crazy kids running past yelling "Hoo-ee!"

Maybe she would take up painting, Rosemary thought. "Great Woman Painter Inspired by Country Residence. Colors of the woods and fields reflected in her calm paintings," her biography would read. That would take care of the dreaded question "And What Do *You* Want To Be?" Nicholas knew; he was going to study fossils. Rosemary hated that question and was amazed at kids who answered, "A doctor, a painter, a truck driver, an actress," just like that. How could you know what you wanted to be when you still had baby teeth in your mouth?

Rosemary took a deep breath. She would practice answering that horrible question. "A painter," she whispered to Freddy. Then, "A writer. I want to be a writer." Her biography would read, "Sensitive Writer Nurtured by a Country Childhood." She would tell them about lying in the field and watching spring come to the tall trees and how

26

that made poems start inside, like bubbles in champagne. Rosemary sat up. She liked that. Was that how poems started, like a sort of fizzy burp that popped out? If she were a writer, then Dad would be proud of her. Words were so important to him. They were important to her, too, but he didn't know that. He didn't know that words stuck in her mouth like dry crackers she couldn't swallow or cough up.

Rosemary sighed and climbed off the bed. The house was settling about them. All their things were inside, and soon it would feel like a home; the yellow rocker in the corner, the pink-and-green flowered rug by the fireplace. All their things would give off that special smell that said "Morgenthau."

Rosemary looked into Nicholas's room and saw that he was arranging his fossil collection. He didn't even turn around, though she breathed heavily in the doorway. She went outside and found her maroon bike propped against the back shed and swung her leg over it. Down their drive, then left up the hill. She passed a man weeding in front of a house that was as neat as an unplayed-in dollhouse.

Rosemary pedaled past rapidly. Mother always said never to speak to strangers. A brown dog and a chubby boy played Wiffle ball outside a house that looked like a cardboard box being unpacked. He looked up as she went by, waved cheerily, and made a face so ugly her bike wobbled. Two more houses, snug and secure on green lawns, and the road turned into another. Rosemary swung around and rode back, the wind cool in her face; down, down to their drive, then up. Maybe she had imagined that sound in the woods when they first saw the house. Maybe there was nothing to worry about after all. It was ordered, it was calm, here. No houses leaning together with soot ground into them. Here the sunlight bounced off clean clapboards, and the lawns out front were like green handkerchiefs.

Rosemary propped her bike against the back shed. She looked at the barn but did not see the wild cat that lived there. Indoors Dad had started a small fire in the woodburning stove, and Mother and Nicholas sat at the oak table. Everything was in its place.

"Hello," Dad said, "you're back. Anything interesting?"

"A man weeding and a boy playing Wiffle ball." Rosemary grinned. "What are you making?"

"Draw up a chair." Dad waved a spoon. "Everywhere in America tonight people are eating cardboard pizzas and paper macaroni. We are being true Americans!" He set out four mugs and ladled canned tomato soup into them.

"Don't forget the beans, Dad," Nicholas said. "They always taste better heated up on a stove."

"I know." Dad set an opened can of beans to heat on top.

Mother sighed and put her chair closer to the stove. "I love it here—it already feels like home."

28

"Me, too," Nicholas said. "There's finally enough room for my rock collection."

"*And* all my Abraham Lincoln books," Dad sighed.

"Don't say you like it so much," Rosemary cautioned.

"Whyever not?" Mother asked, stretching her feet out to the fire and wiggling her toes.

"Because it's—because." Rosemary searched for the words. It was like trying to catch the slippery blobs of mercury from a broken thermometer.

"Because?" Dad said, almost impatiently.

Rosemary paused and felt her throat closing. She coughed. "Because if it's too perfect—it's not good to have anything be too perfect." She drew her chair closer to Mother's; Mom didn't care if she used words.

"Mmm, I know what she means," Dad said. "Like the Greeks when a baby was born. You'd call it a 'toad' or a 'mouse' to keep the gods from being too jealous."

"How's this, Rosemary?" Nicholas stood up. "It's a sad old place, drafty, and the toilet runs. And there are mice in the attic."

"There are?" Mother whispered.

"Yes, I saw their droppings."

Dad stood up, soup mug in hand. "Terrible roof with the slates falling off. The foundation's probably crumbling and the sills are rotten."

Rosemary sighed and pulled her chair closer to Mother.

29

"That's better. We have to be careful, you know." The words rolled away from her and escaped.

"Why?" Mother put her arm around Rosemary and gave her a comforting little shake.

In the warm circle of her arm, it was hard to say why they should be careful. "We just do—believe me."

"Will this help, Rosie?" Dad scooped some of the beans from his plate, opened the door, and scattered them on the doorstep.

Rosemary smiled. She didn't know why, but it seemed the right thing to do.

"George! What *are* you doing?" Mother laughed.

"Keeping ghosts and evil spirits away. It's an old Roman custom. Beans are spirit food." He closed the door. "Better, Rosie?" He came over and rumpled her hair.

"Yes, better." Then she had it. She finally caught the blob of mercury—the words—under her thumb. Maybe whatever it was that was in the woods—whatever had made that gritty, scratchy sound—would eat the beans and leave them alone.

Mathilda Calls the Bike

They were sitting in the kitchen. She could feel them. She could smell the warmth from them that rose from the fields like a warm red sun. She could almost touch it. Their voices floated over the woods, laughter and pauses where they looked at each other and smiled. Mathilda knew it.

She pressed her hand to her chest and moaned. It was worse than she thought it would be. Their being there. Her being here. Looking for a home. Mathilda grabbed Emily and strode to the window. She ground her fingernails into the rotting sill and peered through the glass. Take something. Empty something from them and fill herself up. She went to the door and looked out.

"Come—to me." The words stalked out. Her unused

voice creaked over the dank forest path, out over the meadow, up to the shed where Rosemary's bike rested.

"Come—I—" Mathilda faltered. "Need—you." An owl woke, shook itself rapidly, and flew away, ears seared by the tone. Chipmunks dove for their holes. Rabbits scampered into thickets and crouched, hearts pounding. Her voice was sharp as a nail on a blackboard, harsh as biting sand in a desert storm.

She peered up the path. No bike in sight. Had she forgotten? All those years of study, all those years of remembering, gritting her insides up and holding the black memories inside until they boiled and bubbled under her skin like a blackened bruise.

"Come," she repeated. The memories coiled out like a long black rope and drew things to her, if she tugged with all her will. "Come!" Slowly, slowly, the bike leaned away from the wall and began to move, gears clicking, turning toward the woods. The voices loud in the kitchen continued. No one saw, no one heard. Slowly, then faster, the bike rolled and bumped over the meadow, crushing yellow flowers, up to the start of the woods where vines hung in a thick curtain. It stopped momentarily, held back by a tangle.

Mathilda hissed and the vines broke apart. The bike wheeled through majestically, spun its wheels on the damp leafy path, in the shallow stream, and came to rest against the side of her cabin.

"There, my lovely, there." The skin cracked around her

32

mouth, and Mathilda sat back, exhausted. She couldn't do everything all at once, for she wasn't sure how much strength she had.

But the bike wasn't enough. She had to have more. Mathilda swung her leg over the bike and wobbled up the path. Each time her foot touched the ground for balance, the leaves burned brown beneath. Up the path, through the tangle of vines, through the meadow. She stopped and rested her aching arms on the bike.

The house shone like a beacon. Light streamed out from the windows, making warm patches on the lawn. Voices floated through the open windows, laughter.

Mathilda ground her teeth and raced soundlessly up to the shed. She dismounted, opened the door silently, and snuck inside. She grabbed a trash bag full of soft things, a box marked "Fragile," something that looked like a tiny stove, and hurried outside.

Swinging her leg over the seat, Mathilda balanced her finds on the handlebars and set off for the woods again.

The ache was stilled inside, and she hummed—a noisy rattling sound—as she rode home.

Chapter 4

Rosemary watched the morning light slip into her new room. First it touched the worn sill, sliding down the wall and across the dark polished floor. Then it lay lightly on her bed like a scarf. It touched the edge of her cheek and shone full in her eyes. Rosemary jumped out of bed and went to the window. She opened it and breathed in.

A robin sang in the linden tree. Everything looked safe and snug. The edge of the red barn around the corner. The green meadow. The garden out front with white and pink flowers. No wild cat in sight. It must hunt at night and lie up during the day.

Softly, Rosemary said the names of everything in sight: "Linden tree—red barn—meadow—flowers—back shed," as if by naming, she could make them safe. As if by naming, no one could take these things from her and make her go back to living in thin houses on rattly streets.

As she named "back shed," Rosemary stopped. Where was her bike? She'd gone for a short ride last night, the first night here, and had propped it against the side of the shed. Dad wouldn't have put it away. He always said, "What am I, your maid? *You* pick your own things up." Maybe Nicky moved it somewhere.

She felt a dark cloud on the edge of her day. She put her cheek against Freddy and sighed. If something had happened to that bike, Dad would never let her forget it. He'd told her she was too young for such an expensive bike. Rosemary pulled things out of her bureau drawer, throwing them onto the floor. She yanked on her favorite white jersey with the red hearts on the front and her blue shorts. Maybe they would protect her from whatever awful things lurked in the corners on this day.

She tried to sneak behind Dad into the kitchen, but he heard her and turned to ruffle her hair. " 'Lo, Rosie. Sleep well?"

"Yes, Dad, and would you please call me Rosemary?"

"Sure, Rosie," he said absentmindedly. "Now where is my Carl Sandburg? Rosemary!" He laughed as she poked him. "Did you sleep well last night, dear? Are you feeling crabby?"

"Of course I slept well." Rosemary inched by him. Her

parents had a thing about sleep that she didn't understand. They talked about it as if it were some treasure, hidden and inaccessible. Of course I slept well, she wanted to say, in my own room with Freddy, under my canopy, with a blue mountain out the window!

"Ah, here's Sandburg!" Dad put a book on the shelf, and Rosemary moved on, knowing he would be there for hours arranging his Abraham Lincoln books. Another person who knew what to do.

In the kitchen, Mother was putting dishes away in tall cupboards.

"Hello, Rosie. Sleep well? How do you like your room?"

"Yes, I slept well, and I wish you'd call me Rosemary. I need a new name for a new place."

Mother turned and put her arms around Rosemary. "I know. It's hard moving to a new town. Do you think a new name will make it easier?"

"It might." Rosemary fiddled with the ends of her hair. "I don't like Rosie. Rosie is large and fat with a red face and she drinks whiskey."

Mother hooted. "Oh, Rosie—Rosemary, your imagination! Here, come with me. Let's have tea together in the living room." She poured out two cups of peppermint tea in the pink cat mugs and took them into the living room.

Rosemary followed, touching the edges of the worn, polished furniture. It felt safe and solid under her fingers. Home. Patches of sunshine lay on the pink-and-green flowered rug. Rosemary sat in the yellow rocker and stuck her foot into one of the squares of sunshine.

Mother sat, curling her legs under her in one swift motion. "Are you worried about the new school?"

Rosemary touched her foot to Mother's knee. "Maybe—it's just that you're so graceful and pretty and I'm small and not pretty and there are all those new people at the new school. You know how they stare when you walk into the room!"

Mother raised her chin. "You are too pretty, Rosemary. In a soft, kind way."

Rosemary thumped her foot on the floor. "But Mom, I don't want to be pretty in a 'soft, kind way.' I want to be pretty in an astonishing, wonderful way."

"Well, maybe you will be, Rosemary. People can get to be astonishing and wonderful, depending on what they do with their lives." She rubbed her nose. "You know, I used to hate the first day of school, too. I always threw up the night before. In fact"—Mom smiled—"I was lucky if I threw up the night before. Once I did it on my desk in second grade. Ooooh," she groaned.

"No! Right there in front of everybody?" Rosemary touched Mother's hair. "Poor you. Did they send you home?"

"Of course—all sticky. And then I had to explain to my mother about being sick and you know how *she* is. 'Sickness is all in the mind, my dear!' "

37

They laughed. Rosemary's grandmother was short and stout and utterly fearless. Cuts were to be ignored; head-aches, explained away. Pains in the tummy were "just nerves." "I don't have nerves, my dear," she'd once said, and Rosemary believed her.

"Maybe the thing to do is try and make a friend *before* school starts," Mother said. "You do have two months before September."

"Nicky won't have any trouble at all making friends. Beautiful people never do."

"Well, Nicky won't have trouble making friends because it's not important to him. You know how cats always know who is allergic and go straight to that person and purr on their laps? Nicky's the same way. It doesn't matter to him, so, of course, people love him."

"It's not fair," Rosemary sighed.

"No, it's not, but you have other things that make people like you."

Rosemary sat up straighter. "I do! Like what? Write it down so I can remember."

"You're small. Sometimes people like people who are small. They aren't threatened by them. You are very quick and you know things others don't and you are kind. Kindness is very important."

"One of Dad's categories," Rosemary muttered.

"What's that, Rosemary? What categories?" Mother leaned against her daughter's leg and sipped tea.

"He has, you know, categories for everything, like signs in a supermarket. Pet food—soda—gum. Dad has names for them, like Kindness to Older People, and Being Nice to New Babies, and Never Kicking Your Dog."

"Oh, Rosemary." Mother jumped up and hugged her. "There are things in you I never knew about. You are so right about your father! Wait till I tell him!"

"Don't tell him. Please! He might think I was making fun of him."

Mother looked at her for a moment. "All right, I won't. But sometimes your father *needs* to be made fun of. Anyway, I don't think you're going to have trouble making friends this year. Especially," she added, "if you don't throw up on your desk."

Chapter 5

Rosemary set her mug on the kitchen table, grabbed a piece of bread, and opened the door. Something was missing. Only a brown wrinkled leaf lay on the steps. The beans. Where were the beans Dad put on the steps last night?

"No breakfast, dear?" Mom asked, following her into the kitchen.

"No, Mom, I'm not hungry."

Mother turned and began to stack the blue dishes into the cupboard. "Honey, have you seen Dad's favorite china teacup? He can't find it anywhere. And I think I lost a bag of clothes."

"A bag, Mom? You don't put clothes in a bag!"

"I do," she said shortly, "and they're gone. But your father says they'll turn up, and that people always lose things when they move."

"Well, I haven't seen them," Rosemary said.

"We'll give them a rest," Mom said, and Rosemary smiled. If a toaster didn't work, Mom said, "Let it rest. It will get better." Or, if a pair of socks were missing, she'd say, "Give them time, perhaps they're sulking." She'd give her bike time to come back from wherever it had gone. But what about those beans? Where had they gone? Rosemary shivered and jumped down the steps.

Nicholas was at the edge of the meadow, digging. He worked carefully, putting spadefuls on a mesh sieve he'd made, and sifting the dirt. She ran up to him.

"Find anything?"

"Not yet, but I will." He laid out two sharp rocks and ran his finger along the edges. "What do you think?" He held one out to her.

Rosemary sniffed it. It smelled of earth and damp darkness. "I can't tell—you're the expert. It could be an arrowhead."

"No." He heaved it far into the field. "Not sharp enough and there are no marks on it."

"Marks?" She crouched and poked her finger into the sifted pile.

"From being shaped with a stone. There have to be little gouge marks along the edges." He knelt beside her and pointed.

41

"Oh." It must be nice, Rosemary thought, to be an expert in something, to have all that knowledge stored away like cans in a cupboard. He had a name—collector, knower of rocks. Dad had a name—historian. Mom had a name—dancer. Only *she* had no special name.

"Nicky?"

"Mmmm." He sifted through the dirt, occasionally holding stones up to the light and squinting at them. Rosemary saw that he had the same happy, absorbed look that Dad had when he put away his Lincoln books.

"Did you do anything with my bike last night?"

"Nope," he murmured, nose deep in a handful of dirt.

"I think I lost my bike." There, it was out, the words "bald as an egg," as Mom would say.

"How could you lose it already, Rosie—Rosemary? And where?"

"What am I, a criminal? Anyone can lose a bike. Remember that set of Grandpa's compasses you lost?"

"That was different." Nicholas sat back on his heels. "Someone stole them at school."

"Well, maybe someone stole my bike, Nicky. I read about a gang of people who lived near a college town—we're near a college town—and this gang stole tons of bikes." She sighed. "But I guess I'd better look for it first. Just in case." She ran to the shed and opened the door.

"Where did you leave it last night after you came back

from your ride?" Nicholas stood just behind her, panting slightly.

"Against the wall of this shed." She felt his breathing and it comforted her.

"Aw, Rosie, you know Dad gets mad when we don't put stuff away." He reached past her and pulled on the light string.

"I know, I know." She poked among some large wrapped packages leaning against the shed wall. "What's in here, Nicky?"

He came over and pulled the brown paper away from the edge. "Dad's gardening tools." He chuckled.

"Oh!" Rosemary laughed. "Remember Dad's garden in our last place?"

"Good tools," Nicky intoned. "A man must have the right kind of tools."

"We practically had to build a shed just to keep all his stuff in. Oh, it's not funny, Nicky. If my bike is gone—"

"Hush, it's not gone," Nicholas said sturdily. "Let's look some more."

They pulled out things from the walls and searched the whole length of the shed. The light from the unshaded bulb bounced crazily off boxes and unpacked bundles. They seemed menacing, sharp-edged.

"Rosemary?" Nicholas's muffled voice came from the far end of the room. "Didn't we unpack a hibachi out here somewhere? Mom wants it for tonight, for chicken teriyaki."

"I guess—I don't remember." Her voice trailed off. "I don't see my bike, Nicky."

He joined her, spiderwebs frosting his hair. "Well, let's try the barn, then. Maybe Dad got soft-hearted and put it away for you."

It was still cool and earthy inside the red building. A barn swallow had built a nest above the door and swooped over them, chittering.

Rosemary jumped back.

"It's all right," Nicholas said. "She's just protecting her young. She won't hurt us."

Rosemary looked up. Just over the edge of the muddy, grassy nest rested four tiny heads. They were mostly wide pink beaks with tufts of gray feathers on top.

Nicholas laughed. "Look at them!" He pulled his mouth wide, squinted his eyes, and Rosemary chuckled.

"I hope that wild cat doesn't get them," she said, and searched the old stalls nearby. Piles of old grain sacks rested in the corner, an ancient currying brush with no bristles was on the floor beside a faded sneaker, but there was no sign of the bike.

"See anything in there?" Rosemary called to Nicholas in the next room.

"Nope. Just bits of old lead pipe and boards."

Rosemary went outside into the sharp sunlight and

44

crouched by the stone foundation. "Here, kitty, kitty, here."
She peered into the earthy dark. No sign of that cat. She
got to her feet as Nicholas came up.

"The bike must be *somewhere*, Rosie—Rosemary. Maybe
Dad did do something with it. You know how absent-
minded he is."

"Maybe." Rosemary smiled at her brother. At least he
was trying to call her Rosemary instead of Rosie. The nicest
thing was, he didn't even ask why, he just *did* it. But that
knowledge didn't keep away the gloom as she trailed back
to the house, framing sentences inside. "The special expensive maroon bike you gave me is lost, Dad. The wonderful
I-didn't-deserve-it present is gone. Your money just went
down the drain, Dad. You're right—I'm too young for
something so wonderful."

"Wait." Nicholas put his hand on her arm. "Don't tell
Dad yet. We'll keep looking and see what we can find. He's
busy in there with his books."

What neither of them said was: "You know how mad he
gets when we lose things. No point in upsetting him—or
us—right now."

"All right," Rosemary sighed, thinking that she'd probably have to get a job to earn back the money for a new
bike. "We'll wait. Maybe it'll turn up. Nicky," she said after
a pause, "those beans are gone—the ones Dad put on the
kitchen steps last night."

"Oh?" He looked longingly at the pile of dirt at the edge of the meadow. "That cat that lives under the barn probably ate them."

"Yeah." Rosemary watched him run over the grass, the light shining on his black hair. "But Nicholas," she wanted to shout, "have you ever heard of a cat that ate beans?"

Mathilda and the Cat

She cradled the cup in her hands, holding it up to the light. Just so—the sunshine shone through the flowered china. Like drinking light from a cup. Mathilda sighed and sat down on the couch beside Emily. That was a good thing to take, and every day she would have her tea in this cup and think about how *he* was missing it and wanting it. She rubbed her middle and hummed.

And those clothes. She had on the soft, warm pants now. They never had things like that when she was a girl. Like a blanket inside something soft and stretchy. It made her feel less crabby.

Mathilda smiled at the pile of goods in the corner. "Look, Emily." She held up the doll to see last night's takings.

Things from town as she'd flown over at midnight. Things that would make people scratch their heads and wonder, "Where did it go? Who could take *that*?"

Mathilda hummed again. Her door was open and a sliver of light lay on the floor. It tugged at her, hurt her inside. What looked like that? What did it remind her of? She went to the door and looked out. Somewhere, long ago, she'd seen light like that. Like something she could walk on and feel safe. And something had lain in that path of light, humming the way she'd done not long before.

"Cat!" spat Mathilda. She'd had one, once. A soft white thing like the insides of these pants she had on. There was a cat that lived under the barn. She knew that, just as she had imprinted on her brain the holes and tunnels of all the animals that lived here. A cat would be company. A cat would be a piece of the past that did not hurt. She opened her mouth and out came a sound that was not harsh and railing, but a high, fluting call. It wavered over the fields and coiled around the barn.

Stiffly, grumpily, the black cat arched its back and stretched. He supposed he'd have to answer the call. It was in his blood. It was in hers. But he'd take his time about it. Slowly he walked down the path, slowly he stepped from stone to stone, slowly he sauntered up the path to the rotting hut.

When he reached the door, he stood in the sunlight and looked in. Not very inviting. No food in sight. Spare furnishings. No warmth or stove or fire. She'd have to do better than that.

Mathilda knelt and held out a hand. "Here, kitty, kitty," she croaked. "Come here."

And slowly, knowing that he could always find better lodgings, the cat came to her and butted his head against her clawed hand.

Bad Times

Johnny Preston sat heavily on a stool at Mrs. Nan's counter. He ordered his usual. "Two eggs, sunny-side up, but not all gummy and hard, Mrs. Nan, and two slices of white toast with the butter right out to the edges, four pieces of bacon, and coffee." He breathed the last word reverentially, sniffing the steam from the cup. Coffee. Was there ever anything as wonderful?

Curling up in bed by your warm wife was almost as wonderful, Johnny mused, sipping. Music from high school was almost as wonderful. Watching your kids not make fools of themselves, that, too, was wonderful. But that first hot scald of coffee down your throat—"Ah!" he sighed and leaned back, easing the sore place in his back.

"Well, all is not as wonderful as you may think!" Mrs. Nan plunked her elbows on the counter.

"It isn't?" Johnny said warily.

"No, sir, no sir. Haven't you lost anything yet? I have, my sister has, most of the other people I know have." She swept one arm wide. The regulars nodded and sighed.

"Yep, lost a garden wheelbarrow. One of them expensive ones with the bicycle tires. Just goes to show—never buy anything expensive in case you lose it!" said a man in blue overalls.

"Yeah," said Neil Baldwin, pushing his hat back. "I lost a set of wrenches from my shed."

"And my kid lost her wading pool," said Phil. "That is really sick when someone steals stuff from a kid."

"Yeah," they murmured together.

Mrs. Nan stared at Johnny until he shifted uncomfortably in his seat. "Well, haven't you lost anything?"

"Umph." He wasn't going to say what he'd lost. It was his business. It had just come in the mail yesterday. He didn't even know if it would work, but all the ads said, "Truck drivers! Ease that aching back! Wear our brace! No one will ever see or know!" And now it was gone, stolen from the shed where he'd hidden it until he had courage enough to tell his wife, Brenda, about it.

Mrs. Nan shook her head and took a swipe at the counter.

"I don't know. I don't like it. I remember my great-aunt Emily's diary saying that sometimes bad things happened to this town."

"What d'ya mean, bad things?" Johnny said irritably.

"Just bad things. Cows getting sick. Chickens dying. Animals disappearing and funny mists—clouds." She waved one ringed hand. "Dark clouds." She seized on the word.

"Sounds like a soap opera," Neil laughed. "Dark clouds come to Woodhaven."

"You may laugh," Mrs. Nan snapped, and turned to throw the french fries into the hot oil. They sizzled and hissed. "You may laugh, but I think bad times are coming."

Chapter 6

It rained. It shuddered on the slate roof. It ran gurgling through the ancient gutters and then took a sideways leap off the end near Rosemary's window. She could see the water arching out and down to the honeysuckle bush below. The rain shook the linden tree leaves and washed the trunk black. Even the grass looked pressed and flattened, as if a giant, soaking dog had slept there all night.

Rosemary knelt by the window, elbows on the sill, and hummed tunelessly. She was not sad it was raining. She could hear grumbles from downstairs—"depressing weather"—"truly disgusting day"—and wondered why it was that grown-ups minded the weather so much. Rosemary was glad it was raining, for it meant she could not search for the misplaced bike. It would have another day to come back from whatever place lost bikes went to.

Rosemary got up and unpacked the last of her books. Dad had helped put her old green bookcase between the two windows on the east side of the room. Rosemary set Harold, the porcelain dog, on top. Beside it she put Maude, the white ceramic cat, though they did not like each other very much. Harold was serious, with dark-brown eyes—like Nicky, Rosemary thought—whereas Maude had a skittish, frivolous look with her whiskers slightly askew and her mouth in a smirk. Rosemary always thought that Maude snuck off at night to drink wine and tell racy stories. But Harold spent his life in libraries sitting in a deep leather chair, thinking deep thoughts.

On the first shelf she put *Harriet the Spy* next to an old copy of *Heidi*, beside all of Laura Ingalls Wilder's books. There were no mysteries. Lucretia Portia, a friend from her old school, had loved mysteries. But as Dad said, "You have to love mysteries with a name like that." Rosemary did not like mysteries or suspense or finding things out only at the end of the book. There were all those long stretches of the book where you waited, teeth on edge, to find out if the person was going to get hurt or lost or saved. Rosemary always leafed to the end to make sure things turned out all right. She suddenly wished she could turn to the end of this book, this year, to find out what happened. Would her bike come back? Would they find happiness in the house where things seemed to disappear and menacing noises came from the woods?

She sat back on her heels and hugged her arms close to her chest. She loved this room. It got better each time she looked, like a piece of chocolate cake that tastes richer and lovelier with each bite. She could never look long enough at the yellow roses on the wall, the white curtains at the windows, and the way the old windows divided up the sky and the trees. Her room in her home.

Rosemary wondered who had lived here long ago. Dad said the wallpaper in her room was quite old, possibly a hundred years old. Maybe somebody small with a tiny, pinched waist and dresses with a hundred buttons slept in this room. And she embroidered samplers and made jam at an early age.

Now she, Rosemary, was here—with no buttons, no tiny waist, and definitely no jam. Who will come after me, she wondered? Will another girl live in this room one hundred years from now?

She picked up a pen and went to a corner of the room. Crouching, she wrote in small, clear letters, "Rosemary Morgenthau, nine years, 1991." Then she drew a minute picture of herself in the center of a rose; a snub nose, straight hair, and a smiling mouth. A rose for Rosemary, she thought, and grinned.

Suddenly she squinted and leaned forward. That rose, there—marked by little squiggly lines. She traced them with one finger; two ringlets around the rose's center, two small eyes, a squinched-up mouth. There was a frilly top to an old-fashioned dress with a long, wide skirt. But the face—though it was lightly sketched, Rosemary thought it was squeezed and unhappy.

She searched for a name under the picture. There was none. She stood and examined all the roses on that wall. There could be another picture somewhere, if she looked hard enough. Her eyes blurred from staring at the yellow roses, and soon she began to see odd things in them; queer dogs with no noses, bald men with cigars, and a malicious cat.

"What're you doing, Rosemary?" Nicholas asked from the doorway.

"Thank you for saying 'Rosemary,' Nicky. You know, I just thought. Are you tired of being called Nicky? Would you rather be Nicholas—distinguished and brave Nicholas?" She smiled, carefully avoiding his question.

"Not really," Nicholas said. "I don't think being brave has anything to do with my name. And I don't mind Nicky. Maybe when I'm forty I'll mind, but that's so far away and old it won't matter by then, anyway. What were you doing with your nose all pressed up against the wallpaper? Try a Kleenex." He chuckled.

She batted at his arm. "I'm thinking of—of redecorating. Something new and different."

"To go with your new name?" He looked at her, smiling.

"That's right." Rosemary closed her mouth. She wouldn't tell him that nothing on earth could make her change this wallpaper, now. The picture in the rose was hers—secret.

"I thought you'd like to see this rock." He held it out to her.

Rosemary examined it. There was a feather perfectly printed, the curved spine and fronds branching off from it.

"It's beautiful, Nicky." She handed it back. "Did you find it in the field?"

"No," he said vaguely, "not there."

She opened her mouth, about to ask *where*, then? Was he going to keep secrets from her and have mysteries she didn't know the end to? But the sound of thumping on the stairs and Dad's loud voice stopped her.

"I don't know why we didn't have the moving men put the mirror upstairs, Marjorie," Dad complained.

Thump—crunch! "Watch out for the wallpaper, George!"

They went into the hallway to see their parents struggling with a large mirror, trying to ease it into the empty bedroom.

"What's that for?" Nicholas asked.

"Dance," Mom answered, her face hidden by the mirror. "Positions—feet—arms."

Rosemary and Nicholas hurried into the spare bedroom first, pushing boxes out of the way to make a clear spot along one wall. With a sigh, Mom and Dad lowered the mirror to the floor and leaned it against the wall.

"Ahhh, my first dance studio, George—the first ever after twelve years of tiny rooms!" Mom stood in front of the mirror and assumed a position, legs out-turned, feet almost at right angles to her body. "Ta-da!" Gracefully, she raised her arms and pirouetted in front of the mirror. Her hair flew after her.

"Beautiful, honey, such clean movements," Dad said.

"I'm glad you have a room for your dance." Rosemary was surprised to discover that Mom had hated the small rooms as much as she had.

"We all have our own rooms for the very first time." Dad smiled. "Mine for my books, Marjorie's for dancing, Nicholas's for his rock collection, and Rosie's for . . ." He paused.

There it is, Rosemary thought, *the problem*. Everyone else had a name, a special tag that said, "dancer, rock collector, professor, writer, whatever." Only she had no tag, no special name.

"Rosemary's room for Rosemary—isn't that enough?" Nicholas said firmly.

"Of course it is." Dad kissed them both. "Of course it is."

But that odd feeling of being unmarked stayed with Rosemary. She had no special name—just as that strange picture on her wallpaper had no name underneath.

Out in the hallway she said to Nicholas, "You know, someone lived here long ago—another little girl."

"Of course, silly, lots of people have lived here, I'd bet."

"No, I mean . . ." The words escaped. There was an image in her mind that said, "Someone sad and pinched with her own meanness and the meanness of others." But she could not say it in words. Then and there Rosemary decided; she would find out who had lived here so long ago and what her name was. She would show Nicky that she knew something. She would show Mom and Dad that she was a serious person—a Rosemary and *not* a Rosie.

"Dad?" she called out. "What do you call a person who goes back and tries to find out things?"

"Where, Rosie? What kind of things?" he called from the bedroom.

"Rosemary, Dad, please! Things from the past," she said.

"Ah, the past!" Dad cried, peering around the door. " 'We cannot escape history,' as old Abe L. used to say. You could be talking about a historian, Rosemary, or a researcher."

Rosemary hugged herself and sighed. She felt like one of those paperweights that had been turned upside down to make the snow fall. And now she was rightside up and everything was sifting down.

That's it. I have my name, now, Rosemary thought. I will be a researcher and find out that sad-looking girl's name.

Chapter 7

A chubby boy stood outside their kitchen door. Rosemary recognized him as the same person who made that face at her when she rode up the hill a few days ago. Dad was at work in his college office in town. "Office! My dear office!" he sang this morning, rumpling Rosemary's hair. Mother was upstairs, dancing, and Nicky was digging in the field. Everyone was doing things that would make them famous or earn them money.

The boy knocked again, and Rosemary opened the door. " 'Lo."

"Did you lose a bicycle?" he said, pulling on his left ear.

Rosemary's mouth dropped open, and the boy pushed past her, into the kitchen.

"I've always wanted to see the inside of this house." He sat cozily at the kitchen table and peered into Mother's coffee cup. "Finest Colombian." He sniffed. "Mother loves coffee, that's how I know." He held out the cup. "I'd like some cocoa, or milk, if you've got it. I need building up, Mother says."

Rosemary looked at him—at his thick blond hair, round face, and round blue eyes. His nose was like the lid of an aspirin bottle. "Building up?" She chuckled. "How about some diet cola?" She opened the refrigerator door and handed him a can of soda.

"All right." He smiled at her. "Diet soda is okay, too, though you probably know its full of chemicals. Gives babies hives or something and makes women fall over with headaches. But don't—" He put out his hand, flipped open the top, and downed half of the can in one gulp. "Don't worry about me! I can take chemicals, you know, because I'm large. It's like adults drinking alcohol. The bigger you are, the more your body absorbs it. Did you know that?" He squinted at her in a friendly way.

"Why don't you sit down?" he went on. "I'm a perfectly nice person to talk to, and in fact, I'm the *only* person on this entire street about your age. Everybody else is either a terrible two or a golden elder." He giggled.

Rosemary sat down and laughed. "A golden elder?"

"That's one of those words they use. You know, when your life's all used up and your feet don't work anymore.

61

'Golden' is supposed to make you feel better."

Rosemary took a deep breath. Talking to this person was like riding a roller-coaster. "Who are you?"

"Ernie. Ernie Benerni. Earnest Ernie, Engaging Ernie, Forever Ernie, and you are Rosemary Morgenthau." He waved his hands as if he had just baptized her.

Rosemary nodded. "How do you get all those names and . . ."

"Talk like a commercial?" he finished helpfully. "Early abandoned childhood. Mother works. Father's gone away. Even the dog, Beaver, works. Not me," he said proudly, examining ten fleshy fingers. "I don't work. I make a point of not working. I watch television. When I grow up I'm going to write commercials and make a lot of money and live on a yacht."

Rosemary took a deep breath. "What did you say about my bike, Ernie?"

"A maroon bike, right?"

"Yes, yes, where is it?" Rosemary asked.

"I'm not sure, but—well, you won't believe me, but I had to come tell you." He pulled hard on his left ear again and rubbed his nose.

"Did you see someone stealing it? Did *you* take it?"

"Why would I do that? And then come tell you about it?" He finished the soda and patted his mouth. "Promise you might try and believe me."

"Okay." Rosemary fidgeted in her seat.

62

"Promise you won't laugh?"

She nodded.

"I saw it moving."

"So who was riding it?" Rosemary grabbed a piece of her hair and twirled it.

"That's just it. No one was riding it. It was going along by itself."

"That's impossible!" Rosemary whispered.

"I thought so, too. But I saw it from my bedroom window a few days ago." He turned the soda can round and round in his cupped hands. "I've thought about coming to tell you this for a few days. I was sure you wouldn't believe me."

Rosemary tried to look encouraging.

"Just before it got really dark, I was watching the woods from my window. And I saw this dark shape wheeling across your field. Thought it was a person at first." Ernie paused and chewed on a thumbnail. "But then I saw it was a bike. Moving along with no one on it."

"Just . . . a . . . bike. Bikes can't move on their own."

"This one did." He tried to laugh. "You think I'm crazy, don't you?"

Was it all part of the same thing, Rosemary wondered. The wind in the tops of the pines when there was no wind? That dry, gritty sound from the woods? The hibachi gone, the teacup lost, the bag of clothes that disappeared?

"It *is* pretty hard to believe," he went on. "I don't even know what's happening, but we've lost a lot of stuff from our garage. Mom's been blaming me—thinks I'm rejecting her for working and getting back by stealing stuff."

"Oh, what nonsense!" Rosemary exclaimed.

He grinned at her. "That's exactly what I said."

"This is . . . this is . . ." Rosemary dug her fingernail into the tabletop. She wanted to say, "Please leave! You're scaring me." But how would she ever find out what had happened to her bike?

"What do you think, Ernie?" Rosemary rubbed her arms. This was worse than the sound from the woods and the lost things.

He looked out the window. "I don't know what to think. They don't teach us about these things in school, not the really important things."

"And what are they?" Ernie would like Dad, she could tell.

"Why people stay married? How can there be so many stars and only one planet with life on it? Why do dogs howl when somebody dies?" He looked at her, and Rosemary thought he was daring her to laugh.

She sighed. "You'd like my father. He wonders about things like that, too."

"Will I like your brother? He didn't even say hello when I went by." Ernie's voice ended on a mournful note.

He wants friends, too, Rosemary thought with a start. "You'll like Nicky. Everyone does. He's so beautiful."

"Well, maybe. But that's not a good reason for liking

someone. Besides, I like you already and you're not beautiful."

Rosemary's head jerked up. "You're not supposed to say that! And you're not especially beautiful, either."

"No." Ernie grinned. "But I'm nice and I am never, ever, boring. And now, let's make a pact. If more stuff disappears from your house, call me." He scribbled his number on a matchbook and handed it to Rosemary. "And I'll call you if we lose more things, too." He rubbed his nose, opened the door, and waved.

" 'Bye, Ernie Benerni," Rosemary said. And she wasn't sure if she felt happy or sad or scared or a strange gray mix of all three.

Mathilda and the Cold

"Poor thing." Mathilda sat Emily on her lap and stroked the yarn hair. "They left you to rot." Left with no hair and no face and no insides for her body.

"Poor thing." That's what they had said about her, so long ago. "No mother, father too fond of drink. Clothes like rags. Hair is never combed, poor thing."

Mathilda spat, and the black cat jumped. He was finding living with Mathilda only a hair better than living under the barn. Her idea of food was pinecone soup. Her idea of a cozy hearth was a faded rag rug. He was getting ready to move on—if only she would let him.

Mathilda hissed. The memories boiled under her skin, blackening and spreading. And as she kept them close, she thought of how cold she'd been all those years. Fires in her house that never started, children who stopped saying hello, and then the cold caves of Laughton's mowing, where she moved after Father's house was seized for debt. There, as she aged and the town changed below, she practiced her art. Stole books from the library and studied. Gathered mushrooms and feckless bats and spiders that had forgotten to be careful. Boiling pots over dried moss and scraping the insides of more dead things than she could count. Testing strong words under the cool light of a new moon. Watching night creatures dip overhead, creeping through the underbrush and calling them to her, one by one.

And then the occasional forays into town. A dog stolen. A horse gone. Pots and pans, skirts and washing on lines taken. A pitcher of milk mysteriously soured.

Once she had given mastitis to all of Farmer Black's cows and made Mrs. Sweeney's chickens come out in a strange red rash. She liked to worry them.

People never visited the high mowing anymore. No one ever put a name to the dark mists that rose from the field on moonlit nights, they just stayed away.

Then, as she aged and her skin wrinkled about her like an old quilt, a bath in the brew of old bats and guano. She had emerged—not exactly young, but something other than old. And now it was time. Her 150th birthday was coming up. This was a time of power and change, a time to take back what was hers.

She would start with cold. Maybe that would get *them* out of her house. They could feel what it was like to have no home and to never be warm. She called the cold up inside her body, creeping through her veins, felt the ice crystals behind her eyes, saw pointed needles of ice protruding through the blackened tips of her fingers. Cold gathering in, like a giant ice cave where nothing lived. Through the door the first chilling tendrils crept, out along the path, out over the green meadow. The yellow flowers on the path withered and bent. The windows in the big house suddenly fogged with cold.

"Go!" Mathilda spat in the cat's ear. "Make them uneasy, give them fleas and shivers."

Slowly, to prove that he still had his own will, the cat waved his tail and sauntered out the door. Up the path, past the blasted flowers, up to the doorstep. Then he paused. Not yet. He was not ready to go into the house just yet. He had a fine sense of his own importance and wished for a more dramatic arrival. He sat behind a dogwood tree to wait, as it began to rain.

Chapter 8

"Cold for the beginning of July." Mother shivered that night on the couch and spread the purple afghan over her knees.

Rosemary made a pile of brittle pinecones in the fireplace. Beside her, Dad laid up some dry apple wood and lit the fire. They sat back and smiled at the orange flames licking through the tinder. Rosemary felt the warmth from Dad's body and leaned closer. He hugged her and said reasonably, "Well, you do sometimes get nights like these in early summer, Marjorie."

Nicholas sat in the far corner, reading a book on fossils and comparing the rock in his hand with the book's pictures.

"Look!" He stood up suddenly. "I bet this is from the

Jurassic period!" He ran over, waved it in Rosemary's face, and then showed it to Dad.

"What's the Jerry—Jerra—?" Rosemary asked.

"A period in history," Nicky said impatiently. "Far away and long ago."

"Don't be so smart, Nicky!" Dad looked up at him. "I really hate it when you talk like that. It makes people feel small and unimportant and makes you look all puffed up."

"But—" Nicky looked at the fossil.

"No buts! Answer your sister."

"The Jurassic period runs from 180 million to 135 million years ago and was characterized by dinosaurs and conifers," Nicky intoned.

"All right, all right." Rosemary tucked her heels under her. "I get the point. I guess we could say you're excited, right?"

"Yes, I am excited, Rosie—Rosemary, sorry."

He ruffled her hair in passing and sat down with his book. "This land is just *full* of fossils! It's the best place we could've chosen. Lake Hadley used to be here, you know."

"Hadliloveya, Hadliloveya," Dad sang off tune and shoved another log onto the fire.

"And there are dinosaur tracks down in the valley, too." Nicky began to read again.

"Ain't history grand?" Dad smiled at them. "I know what you mean, Nicky. This house just *leaks* history. I can imagine the slaves going North and staying here—in this very house.

Sometimes I think I can hear their feet in the attic."

"Don't!" Rosemary put her hand on Dad's knee. "That's scary. I don't want anybody from the past in my house!"

"You may not want them," Dad said, "but they may be here."

Rosemary shivered and pulled her sweater closer. Could whatever took her bike, the hibachi, Mom's clothes, and Dad's teacup be something from the past?

"Remember," Dad said, standing up, " 'We cannot escape history,' as old Abe used to say."

"Well, I wish we could escape this cold!" Mother said. "It's not right for it to be so cold."

Blasts of air shook the old windows, and they rattled in their frames. The rug puffed in one corner and something wailed outside.

"The cat, George." Mother turned her head toward the window. "It's that wild cat that lives under the barn. Maybe it wants to come in. Rosemary, go and see if it's at the door."

"But Mom . . ." Rosemary did not want to leave the bright fire, the safe circle.

"I'm surprised at you, Rosemary. You're usually the first one to pick up a smushed blue jay by the side of the road. Remember what we used to call you?" Dad grinned as they said together, "Our Lady of the Lost Animals. Scoot! Kindness to Animals is very important."

There it was again. One of Dad's categories. Next to

71

Helping Elderly Women and Comforting Crying Babies, Being Kind to Animals was high on Dad's list.

Slowly, Rosemary got up and went through the cold study to the kitchen. The fluorescent light over the sink made the kitchen look like a moonscape. Rosemary peered through the door window. It was completely black outside.

"Open the door, Rosie!" Dad's voice came from the living room.

She jumped at a touch on her shoulder. Nicky stood behind her.

"It's a little spooky out there, isn't it," he said comfortably, opening the door. The night blew around them. Trees rattled and shook, and the wind and rain ricocheted around the house. Something squealed nearby and Rosemary slammed the door.

"What is it, Nicky? Oh, what *is* it?"

It came again, a high-pitched squealing, and Nicky stepped closer to the door. "Don't know. I can't see." He pushed the door open a crack and looked out. Suddenly he jumped straight up in the air and a dark shape shot past him. It ran through the study and into the light. Nicky ran after, but Rosemary stayed behind, clutching her sweater and making up chants.

"Don't—let—it—be—anything—scary—or—hurting."

"There, you see?" came Mother's comforting voice. "Heat up some milk, will you Rosemary? This cat's half starved."

"There, there," Dad crooned, and Rosemary could see

him crouched over a dark, matted shape on the hearth. It looked pitiful, with plastered coat and drooping whiskers. Its tail lay limply behind.

Rosemary hurried to warm some milk and brought it in a little blue dish. She set it down before the cat, who sniffed it, stepped back, paused, and then lowered its head to drink steadily, greedily, until the last drop was gone.

"There, will you look at that?" Dad sounded as pleased as if he'd just fed and burped a baby. "Now things'll be better," he sang to the cat. "Now things'll be better." He stroked it softly.

"Nicky, will you please bring me a towel?"

He raced upstairs and came back with a green towel. Dad lifted the cat carefully and set it down on the towel. "We'll let it dry by the fire."

Rosemary watched carefully. Something. There was something about it she didn't like. The way it curled up on the hearth as if it owned it. The way it lifted one eyelid and looked slyly at Dad and Mother, weighing them with a quick, sideways glance. The way its wet tail lifted and dropped, lifted and dropped. It yawned and kept its yellow eyes wide open, something Rosemary had never seen a cat do.

She felt a cold breath on her neck, and she shivered. Everyone seemed to be enjoying the spectacle of a fed, warm cat on their hearth. "Don't," she began and stopped. They all looked at her and did not see how the cat ruffed its fur out the wrong way so it stood out like a thick, black burr. It was suddenly terrifying and fierce, its legs swelled to twice their size and its head huge and bristling. Then it pulled the fur flat against its body again—suddenly dry.

"See?" She pointed. "Did you see what it just did?" Rosemary stepped back and rubbed her arms.

"See what, Rosie?" Dad said.

"See . . ." She sat in a chair, and her mouth seemed to close in upon itself.

"Words, Rosie," Dad said impatiently. "Use words."

She looked at Nicky. He had not seen it. In the country where Nicky lived, there was no such thing as a cat that could push all its fur out. He smiled encouragingly at her, and she frowned. He couldn't help.

If I use words, she wanted to say, you won't believe me. And I can't put it into words anyway. Suddenly she thought of Ernie. He would have noticed that startling, black fur standing out as if an unseen hand had rubbed it, hard.

Chapter 9

Rosemary picked up the phone and dialed. She could hear Mother and Father talking downstairs and the snap of pine resin from the fire. Nicholas was talking to the cat about warm beds and fires and bowls of hot milk.

"Ernie?" Rosemary whispered.

"Yes! Something's happened?"

"Well, maybe. I don't know."

"Tell me. What is it? Something else disappeared from your house? Mother lost an old gray scarf yesterday, something her mother had knitted for *her* years back. It was very ugly, as I kept telling her, but she feels pretty sad about—"

"Ernie, hush a second. It's a cat. It came in out of the

darkness and the wind and rain tonight. It made a strange sound."

"Like aliens?" Ernie said helpfully.

"Something like that. And it's sitting—lying—on our hearth like it owns it."

"But all cats are like that, Rosemary." Ernie sighed.

"This is different. It kept looking at everyone, not at all the way a cat does. More like a—a— I don't know." Words escaped her. "And then after Nicky dried it with a towel and we fed it warm milk, when no one was looking, it pushed its fur out."

"How do you mean, pushed its fur out?" Ernie tapped his fingers against the phone. It made it harder to go on.

"Ruffed it out—you know—how a dog does . . ."

"When it doesn't like you?" Ernie finished for her.

"Yes, but not just its tail—the whole fur all the way around, even on its legs." Rosemary sighed. "I know it doesn't sound like much, Ernie, but you said to tell you if anything happened and I think this is an anything."

"All right, Rosemary, I believe you. If you say it's an anything, then it must be."

He believed her! She didn't have to explain, dragging words out of her like old bulky packages and trying to arrange them the right way. He was a friend—the one she'd been hoping for.

She sighed again. "Thanks, Ernie. Now what?"

"Just keep an eye on it—her—him. See where she—he—

it goes. Take notes. Show them to me tomorrow. And Rosemary—" She stopped just as she was about to hang up the phone. "Don't be frightened."

"I'll try," Rosemary said and thought of Freddy. Now was a good time to get in under the blue quilt, put her cheek against Freddy, and read something really safe and comforting, like *Little House on the Prairie*, or maybe *Little House in the Big Woods*, where Pa and Ma could always make everything come right, and the wild animals were mostly far away, and the light from Pa's fire shone cozily on Laura's and Mary's faces.

Cold and Foggy

Neil Baldwin pulled his hat up. "Cold, ain't it?" He waved his coffee cup at the five other customers at Mrs. Nan's counter.

"Mmmmph," murmured the regulars. "Sure is cold for July. Can't work on my house today. It's too cold and foggy."

Mrs. Nan dished out eggs with a flourish. "It's a frontal attack or something."

"Front, front, Mrs. Nan," Neil corrected her. "Cold front meeting . . ."

"I know that, I know that." She thumped the eggs down. "Cold meets warm. Equals fog. No vision. Accidents. Bad tempers, too, I might add." She glared at Neil. If there was anything she hated, it was being corrected. Didn't she watch the weather station each night from eleven to eleven thirty? Didn't she listen to John Quill each morning and see the clouds rotate on the weather map? It was always so reassuring to know what was happening as it was happening.

"Whew, cold and foggy!" Johnny Preston blew in the door, his big ten-wheel truck parked out front. "Been on the road all day, and I ain't never seen weather like this. Pea soup is what it is."

"Yeah, pea soup," muttered the five at the counter.

"Where does it come from, I'd like to know," said Johnny.

"Up north." Neil jerked his head. "Arctic weather drifts down our way."

"Well, I wish they'd *keep* it up north, that's what I say." Johnny sat down with a bump and pushed his hat back. He saw equally badly with his hat up or down, and this cold and fog had confused and frightened him. If his eyesight was going, if he couldn't drive his rig, how could he earn a living?

"Smells a little funny, too?" Phil offered, his face deep in a coffee cup.

"Mmm, musty," Neil said, wiping his mouth.

"Like when the wind's from the dump," Johnny said.

"Well, whatever it is, wherever it's from, whatever it's

called, we don't want it, that's what!" Mrs. Nan plunked her elbows on the counter and glared from under penciled brows.

"Hear, hear," the men murmured. "You make it go away, Mrs. Nan. You take care of it."

"Well, maybe I will." She pushed her hair back and took a swipe at the counter with her rag. "Maybe I will."

That long gray scarf. That should do. Carefully, Mathilda wound it around her head and tucked the loose end under. She put on a pair of dark glasses, the silver kind that reflect the world. She pulled on the raincoat she'd found in the Salvation Army box, tied her high red lace-up sneakers, and looked in the cracked mirror. She could see herself in the lenses of her glasses, and she smiled.

Outside, she wheeled the maroon bike out from under the cabin's eaves, where she'd hidden it. She patted the seat. Nice, these machines. Far nicer than the bicycles of her girlhood—huge things with scary, great wheels and tiny pedals. If you fell off, which she did a lot, it was a terrible, long way down. She threw one leg over the bike and wobbled up the forest path. No one saw the strange, bundled figure emerge from Rosemary's woods. No one saw her ride precariously across the field, out onto the road, and down the hill past the graveyard. In the cold fog she seemed just a denser patch of cloud.

"Three o'clock! It's not three o'clock!" She spat at the church clock as she passed, and suddenly it began to move. Its arms swung round rapidly and settled at five, the true hour. It began to bong, but Mathilda just pointed and it stopped. How she hated that noise. She used to hear the church bells from her house when she was young, and later from her high, damp cave. Bells, calling people together. People sitting together and talking—not like her alone in her flowered room.

She pedaled over the bridge, sniffed appreciatively at the river, and cycled past the stone library. She had no difficulty seeing in the fog. Down past the brick school, past the old horse fountain with geraniums planted in the middle.

"Zap!" She pointed at the flowers and they shriveled and turned brown. Down route nine, past the schoolhouse. Mathilda stopped and leaned the bike against the air. The old school was gone. This was new, brick and paint and great slashes of glass with flowers pasted on them. Mathilda hissed and all the flowers dropped to the floor. She swiveled her head. That was the old playground. Only now it was covered with strange shapes. A sort of ladder. A shining piece of something that went from a high place to a low place. A sandbox. And children playing.

Their voices were high and sweet. Mathilda pressed her hands to her ears. Someone laughed and called. Another called back. Three children determined to play, despite the fog, were dressed in slickers and jeans, running and shouting. A small boy in a red jacket shot down the slide. A girl in a yellow slicker raced up the ladder and stood at the top, waving. "King of the mountain!" she shouted. "King of the mountain!" A third boy in a blue raincoat bounced on a platform. A little dog hurried and yapped, keeping them all safe with his quick feet and bristling tail. A mother in a wet scarf waited patiently on a bench.

Mathilda sucked in her lips and looked. Her eyes turned yellow, burning out of her face like fog lamps. Suddenly the girl shot down the slide and it collapsed behind her. The slide rose into the air, reversed itself, and came down like a drifting leaf. The boy in red started to climb the ladder and then fell two steps to the ground as the ladder flew into the air. The boy in blue jumped off before the platform under him pulled out of the ground. All the pieces of the playground rose in a lazy spiral, circled, and flew off toward the woods, leaving a bare, worn space marked by children's feet. The dog barked hysterically, running in circles, licking the three children. The mother jumped to her feet and ran toward the children, shouting, "Are you all right?"

"Home!" the girl in yellow cried. "I want to go home, Mommy."

"A tornado!" panted the boy in red. "That's what it was."

"Yes, a tornado," the woman said uncertainly. She hugged all three children and made them hold hands.

"No," said the other boy, "not a tornado, but I don't know what." They set off, the dog following close to their heels.

Mathilda mounted her bike again, patted her hair, and rode off home to the woods, feeling a sensation so akin to happiness she did not know what it was.

Chapter 10

Rosemary peered out the kitchen window. The air was a cold, gray smear. Water lay on the grass and the trees, clouding the windows. Her hair lay flat against her neck. Through the window she saw Nicholas, dressed in his yellow slicker, obstinately digging in the wet earth. In the next room Mother stretched while Dad watched. Rosemary could hear the *pop* of joints cracking.

"Wretched weather," Mother said. "First it was cold, now it's wet, George. I know New England is changeable, but this is ridiculous. It's the beginning of July."

"I know, dear," murmured Dad. Rosemary could see him through the open door. He was sitting on a tall stool, sipping the third of his four cups of morning coffee. "I just can't seem to get going this morning. At least the cat is awake," he said fondly, as the black cat arched and purred by Dad's foot.

"I don't like that cat!" Rosemary said loudly.

"Whyever not?" Dad called back. "He's a lovely little beast with a beautiful coat."

"He's not lovely and he isn't little!" Rosemary said. "And you'll be sorry." She scratched her arm. There were four little red bumps.

Dad came to the doorway, puzzled. "Sorry for what, Rosie?"

"Rosemary, Dad." She stirred her cereal. The words rolled away under Dad's scrutiny.

He sighed.

"Fleas, Dad." She seized on the word. "I think he has fleas. I've got bumps."

"Well, that's easy to fix, Rosie." Dad came into the kitchen and took a seat. "But what could we have to be sorry about, helping that poor old cat?"

"He's not poor or old," Rosemary said slowly. "There's something strange about him."

The cat sat by Dad's foot, butting its head against the leather shoe.

Dad scratched the animal's ears. "Strange how?"

So many questions! Why couldn't he just believe her, the

way Ernie had on the phone last night? With Dad waiting
for an answer, Rosemary was more than glad to see Ernie's
comforting, squashed face at the kitchen door.

"Come in!" She jumped up and opened the door. "Come
in. Dad, this is my friend Ernie." Nicholas followed just
behind.

Ernie held out his hand. "Ernie Benerni, Mr. Morgenthau. Welcome to Woodhaven. It's a small town, but it's
full of character, even though it's a bit cold and damp."

Dad grinned. "Thanks, Ernie. Are you running for office?"

Ernie smiled back, not at all offended. "Nope. Maybe
Rosemary told you; I'm planning a career in television and
that's how people are there. They hold out their hands a
lot, did you notice?"

Mother came in, pulling up her dance tights.

Dad chuckled. "Yes, I noticed. Ernie, this is my wife,
Mrs. Morgenthau, my son, Nicholas, and now I'm off
to get some work done, cold or no cold, damp or no
damp!"

Nicholas nodded, saying, " 'Lo," as he pulled off his wet
slicker and sat at the table.

Mother wiggled her toes and stretched out one leg. Rosemary was embarrassed, but also proud. Other mothers were
round with square bottoms. When they bent over in the
supermarket, you hoped no one would see. Her mother was

86

slim and lean as a race horse, and she looked hardly old enough to have two children.

"Hello there, Mrs. Morgenthau." Ernie held out his hand and shook Mother's firmly. "I live up the street. The tiny house with the red shutters. One beagle dog, Beaver, and one mother, divorced. Mrs. Smith."

Mother smiled. "How nice to meet someone who shakes hands."

"Yes, well, as I told your husband, if I'm going to go into television, I'll have to shake hands a lot, won't I?" He plumped himself down at the table and looked expectantly at Rosemary. "Perhaps cocoa?"

"Yes, cocoa, Rosemary," Nicholas said. "I'm all wet and grumpy from being outside. And I didn't find one thing!"

Somehow Rosemary didn't mind Ernie asking for food. It was part of his being soft and comfy, having a squashed nose, and using made-up names. She turned the heat up under the kettle.

"What were you looking for?" Ernie asked.

"Oh, things," Nicholas said vaguely.

"Not things, Nicky!" Rosemary said, her back to him as she poured hot water onto the cocoa. "Tell him."

"Arrowheads. Fossils," Nicholas mumbled.

Rosemary started, realizing that Nicky was shy about what he did, afraid that even comfy Ernie might make fun of him.

87

"That's neat," Ernie said. "I know someone at school who does that, collects things, stones and fossils and the beautiful skinny fish you see in those old stones."

"Thanks, Rosemary." Nicky set the hot cup down. "Yeah, those. I'd love to find one of those fish."

"Oh, good," Ernie said, taking the mug of cocoa from Rosemary. "I love this kind. You can chew on the marshmallows. Have you been exercising?" he asked Mother. "My mom always tries to do those TV exercise shows, and then she eats a baloney sandwich afterward. Do you do that?"

Mother laughed and sat down at the table. "No, I've been practicing dance, as you can see from my tights."

Ernie scratched his nose. "Well, you might just have cold legs—like my mother."

"Oh, I'm a dancer all right. Do you know how you can tell?"

Ernie shook his head.

"My feet, that's how." Mrs. Morgenthau propped one foot on the table.

"Mother!" Nicholas and Rosemary said together.

"It's all right, Ernie doesn't mind, do you?" He shook his head. "See these knobby bits, here and here? That's from early toe work."

"Early toe work?" Ernie giggled.

"Dancing *en pointe*, up on my toes. Really, it's a stupid way to dance. It just kills your feet, but when you're young, that's all you want to do."

"And now you don't?"

Rosemary put her arm around Mother's shoulder. How did Ernie know to talk to adults this way? He was like someone on a soap opera, meeting a friend in a bar and having a conversation over white wine.

"No, I don't, Ernie." Mother sighed. "I just want to dance well, move well, and use this body while it lasts. But no silly stuff like staggering around on my toenails!"

Ernie laughed and sipped his cocoa. He stirred it with one pudgy finger. "What do you think of this fog, Mrs. Morgenthau?"

"Not much! First it was freezing, now this." She spread her hands and examined them. "It makes my bones ache."

"And I can't dig in my meadow," Nicholas grumbled.

"Well, it's all part of it, you know." Ernie stopped smiling.

"Part of what?" she asked.

"Oh, all the things we've lost, the cold, that smelly fog."

Rosemary glared at him. He wasn't going to tell Mother about the lost bike!

"And what's that all part of, Ernie?" Rosemary could tell Mother was humoring him.

"I'm not sure. But whatever it is, it lives in your woods."

Almost on cue, Nicholas and Mother rose at the same time. "I've got to go upstairs," Nicholas said. "Nice to meet you, 'bye."

And Mother stretched, saying, "Next you'll be saying it's ghosts and goblins. I've got to get back to my practicing. Nice to meet you, Ernie." She waved and left the room.

"Actually," he said to her disappearing back, "I think it's a witch." But Mother did not hear. "A witch, Rosemary." He turned to her.

She sat down suddenly. "How do you know? And there's no such thing as witches, anyway, Ernie!"

"There isn't? Who says? A textbook in school? I wonder if your father would believe in them. I can see your brother doesn't." He stood. "Maybe I'll go ask."

"No, no! Sit down! Don't ask Dad. He can be—funny," she said. "We'll do this on our own. How do you know it's a witch?"

"I think I saw her," Ernie said, sipping his cocoa. Then he choked and sputtered. "Oh, Rosemary, it wasn't at all funny or like those movies on TV. No weird music in the background, nothing to tell you this was it. Just the dark coming in. I was watching from my window and I saw this, this person, I guess, riding your bike. Riding it badly, I might add." He stopped and fiddled with the cup's handle.

"What did she—it—look like?" Rosemary whispered.

"Like somebody in hiding. All bundled up in a shabby coat with mom's gray scarf and some weird silver sunglasses."

"But maybe it was just a homeless person," Rosemary said hopefully.

"No. Her eyes, they weren't like a person's eyes. They glowed yellow even through the glasses. And she smelled, Rosie, I could smell her all the way across the field. And it wasn't the not-having-a-bath-for-two-weeks kind of smell."

Rosemary waited.

"Like how an old chicken smells after being in the garbage for three days."

Rosemary clutched her stomach and wished she had Freddy right beside her, right this minute.

The words bunched up in her throat. She stood and pointed to the cat lying in a square of sunshine. "It—came. The one I told you . . ."

". . . about," Ernie finished for her. He knelt by the cat and peered into its face. Suddenly he stepped back, startled.

"The eyes, Rosie. The same eyes, like headlights."

Rosemary moaned. "And no one else sees but us."

The cat rose lazily to its feet and circled the table, once, twice, three times.

"Get out," Ernie whispered. He ran to the door and opened it, shoving the cat out with his foot. "Out!"

"Oh!" Rosemary sat with a bump at the table. "That was brave. I'm never brave, Ernie. Thank you for making it go away." She put her head in her hands and wished for it to all disappear, this minute. The—whatever it was that was in her woods—the cat, the damp cold, the missing things, everything.

"I don't like it." Ernie sat beside her and patted her hand.

"What?"

"She—he—it circled us, once, twice, three times. I don't like that at all."

The Regulars

"Sicko." Phil Townsley choked on his coffee. He slapped the newspaper with one hand, and the headline, Vandals Destroy Woodhaven Playground, bounced.

"Yup, truly sicko." Neil Baldwin swung one booted foot against the stool.

"A playground. How could anyone do that to a playground?" Mrs. Nan had tears in her eyes.

"*Our* playground," Johnny reminded her as he sat at the counter. He knew he couldn't stay long; his rig was idling on the roadside. But he had to have that jolt of coffee, and he had to talk to someone about what had happened.

"Yeah, we built it," Phil said. "I personally killed one

thumb putting that slide up." He held out a misshapen thumb.

"*Who* would do such a thing?" asked a man in jogging sweats and blue shoes. The regulars turned briefly in his direction and then swung back to Mrs. Nan.

"Who knows?" Neil shrugged. "Even in a small town like this you get some sick people."

"It's not sick." Johnny set down his cup, hard. "How about evil? I'm tired of every time something bad happens it's 'sick.' When I was a kid, the word was 'wrong,' or 'bad.'"

"Yeah," said Mrs. Nan, smoothing her hair back. "I think we could call this 'evil.' It doesn't seem like a prank or somebody out just blowing off steam."

"Hah." Neil nudged Johnny. "I remember the way *you* used to blow off steam when we were in high school. That car of yours. Whoo!"

Johnny stuck his nose into his cup. He didn't like to be reminded of how wild he'd been, now that he was settled down with two growing children. Only a bent nose told of that terrible accident and the wild drive that led up to it.

"Yeah, evil." He shifted in his chair. "And the strangest thing is, nobody's found where the playground stuff went. It just disappeared. Gone."

The stranger in the jogging suit got up to pay for his breakfast. He jingled the coins in his pocket and said, "It's probably some kid who had a rough life, a bad father, you know."

No one answered as Mrs. Nan doled out his change, and he pushed open the door.

"Huh, a bad father. I'll show you a bad father," Phil said. "This is wickedness, that's all."

"Yeah." The rest nodded, finished their coffee, and went out to their idling rigs and work trucks. Only Mrs. Nan was left, polishing the counter. Seized with an inexplicable urge, she began to scrub in corners long forgotten. She poured white vinegar through the coffee maker and got out the Brasso. At least *her* corner would shine.

Chapter 11

Rosemary knelt by the drawing on her wallpaper. There was the girl's collar, an uncertain, wavering line. There were the two ballooning marks that formed her skirt. She counted the twelve tiny dots that were the little girl's buttons. And two corkscrew curls must be her hair. But her mouth. How could one line be so sad and disappointed? Maybe all the damp and cold had been here when the little girl was alive, and that made her look sad and disappointed.

Could there have been— Rosemary stopped and sat back on her heels, reaching for Freddy with one hand. But the word jerked across her mind. Could there have been—a witch, then? She tried not to think of Ernie's words, but they'd stayed and repeated themselves over and over. "I think it's a witch, Rosemary." "Her eyes, they weren't a person's eyes."

Outside her door Nicky sang, " 'Oh my darling, oh my darling Clementine.' "

Slowly, she put Freddy back on the bed, gave him a last pat, and followed Nicholas downstairs. She looked around for the cat and sighed happily when she didn't see it.

"Nicky?" She trailed her hands along the wallpaper, small Chinese houses with scooped boats and weeping willows. He turned.

"Do you think there's something wrong with this house?" She spoke softly so Mother and Dad would not hear from the kitchen. She didn't want to give them any ideas.

"How do you mean, wrong?" he asked.

"Oh, my bike going—we haven't found it yet, you know, and Dad's china teacup and Mom's stuff and all this cold and damp and that cat appearing out of the night. Like that, Nicky." She sat on the carpeted step and looked at him.

He sat, facing her, and she felt comforted. Maybe he would help.

"I don't think those things mean anything," he said reasonably. "A little bad weather, and we've just moved house. Stuff disappears when people move."

"Mmm-hhmmm. But what if it's—what if it's"—the words stopped and then popped out—"a witch, Nicky?"

He started. "A witch? What makes you think that, Rosie—Rosemary? And we don't believe in them, anyway. Science doesn't either," he said firmly.

"I know *you* don't, and I know science doesn't." She tugged miserably at her socks. "I was just wondering. Of course it's not a witch," she said and rose. "I was just teasing, Nicky." But the odd thing was, her denying that it was a witch made it seem all the more likely that it *was* a witch.

He looked relieved and bounded down the steps. "I'll help you look for your bike again, Rosemary, after breakfast if you like."

"Thanks." She wanted to touch his back as he went away from her, but she couldn't reach him. Maybe that little girl on the wallpaper hadn't had a brother. Maybe that was why her mouth was sad and disappointed.

Dad was sitting at the kitchen table, sipping coffee and munching on a bagel. He shook the paper and Rosemary started. "Look at this!" he said. "Some vandal destroyed the new playground by the school. Now who would do such a thing?"

"Who, indeed?" Nicky said, pouring raisin squares into a bowl. "That is really sick, doing in a kids' playground. That is just the lowest of the low. Is it as bad as vandalizing a cemetery, Dad?"

"Mmmm." He considered the problem. "Disrespect for the Dead versus Not Caring for Children. What do you think, Marjorie?"

While they debated the problem, the words echoed in Rosemary's head: "the lowest of the low." It was the sort of thing a witch would do—destroy something that was built just to give fun. Could Ernie be right?

"I think that ruining the playground is worse," Dad said. "It's the living that matter."

"My joints matter," said Mother. "I wish this weather would change. I feel like an eighty-year-old woman!"

"I know. I'm going into town today to rent a dehumidifier and get some flea spray for that cat. I'm afraid my books will get damaged if this damp keeps up."

"Good thing fossils don't mind damp," Nicky said, reading his book.

Rosemary eyed the three of them warily. They were disappointed. Sad and disappointed like that little girl's mouth. The house was not turning out the way they had hoped. All their dreams of firefly nights and ghost stories on the porch were turning wet and soggy.

Maybe they'd want to sell the house. Maybe they'd have to go back to living in Garden City. Just for one moment a week ago, she'd wanted to go back. It had been ugly and sour there, but at least she'd known what made it ugly. Sad people. Dirt. Too many cars. Grime in the air.

"You're not," she began and stopped. "You're not—"

"Yes, Rosie—Rosemary?" Dad smiled.

"Not thinking of—" she couldn't force the word out.

"Leaving?" Dad said. He came over and put his arm

around her. "No, honey, we're not thinking of leaving. We still love this house. It's just—"

Mother interrupted. "If only we had a cleaning woman, George! Then we could blame all the things we've lost on her!"

"We couldn't blame the weather on her," Nicholas said reasonably. "And what have we lost?"

"One hibachi and a cooking pan," Mother ticked off on her fingers. "One whole box of large garbage can liners. Dad's army poncho he used for watching birds. A bag full of my exercise clothes, and Dad's special china teacup with the roses around the rim."

And a bike, Rosemary thought.

"And a bike," Nicholas said aloud, looking at his sister. She kicked him under the table.

"A bike? What's this, Rosie?" Dad gave her shoulder a little shake. "Your bike is gone?"

Rosemary concentrated on putting three Nabisco squares on her spoon.

"When did you lose it?" Dad asked. The lines deepened around the sides of his mouth.

Maybe he would pay attention, Rosemary thought. Maybe he would fix whatever was wrong.

"The day we moved here—over a week ago," Rosemary mumbled.

"Why didn't you say anything then?"

"Because—because—"

Dad patted her shoulder and she stopped talking. She couldn't say "Because I was afraid, because maybe a witch stole it."

"Maybe she can't finish her sentences because we keep going on at her, George," Mother said. "Because why, Rosemary?"

"Because I was afraid Dad would be angry," she said in a small voice.

Dad kissed her loudly and sat down again. "I'm not angry, honey! That's what happens when people move house. Things disappear. It'll turn up, you'll see."

"Where is it that all the lost things of this world go to?" asked Mother. "Rhode Island, or is it New Jersey?"

Dad laughed. "We'll put an ad in the paper, and have a good look around. What are your plans for today, Rosie?"

"Would you please call me Rosemary? This is a new house, a new town, and I need a new name. Something— bigger." She thought of that tiny girl on the wallpaper and wondered if she had had a small name that didn't fit anymore. Suddenly, she remembered what she'd decided to do. "I'm going to do some research at the library. I am going to be a researcher, and those kinds of people are not called 'Rosie.' "

He chuckled and she grinned back. "Okay, Rosemary, but you know, I'm going to miss your old name. It feels like the time you gave up nursing when you were little."

Mother sighed in agreement. "I hated it when you stopped nursing."

"You did? Why?"

"It was so cozy," Mother said. "You pressed up against me with your warm, soft little body and I'd fill you up with milk while Dad read to me."

"That sounds nice," Rosemary said, though she could not imagine ever being so small that she nursed.

"And then you gave up your bottle and got bigger and talked more and suddenly you were a girl, not a baby, not a toddler."

"So that's why I hate to see 'Rosie' go," Dad said.

Rosemary came over and hugged him. "Then you can call me Rosie if you really want, but everybody else,"—she looked at Mother and Nicky—"has to call me Rosemary." She left the kitchen, ran up the hall stairs, and picked up the phone.

"Ernie?"

" 'Lo, Rosemary. What's up?"

Rosemary could hear Beaver whuffing in the background and some off-key singing.

"I'm walking down to the library—want to come?"

"Sure, but what for? What are we going to do there?"

"I want to find out who lived here long ago. I didn't tell you before, but there's a picture on my wallpaper of a little girl—a long-ago girl."

"And?" he said helpfully.

"And I want to find out who she was. Maybe the witch was here when the girl was here, Ernie. I don't know. It's just a hunch."

"So you agree it is a witch?" He paused.

"I guess. I don't know. But we can find out."

"Okay. I like hunches. I'll be right over and we can go down together." He hung up the phone.

Rosemary set it down on the table. "Together." What a lovely word. It almost canceled out her worry about the house, the woods, and that cat.

When she ran downstairs, humming, she stood in the kitchen doorway looking out over the meadow and the tall grass beaded with moisture. Swallows dipped above the grass and swung high again, chittering. A cow lowed through the fog. And it was only as she put her foot down on the first step that she saw three mice with their heads cut off, arranged as neatly as asparagus on a plate.

Chapter 12

Ernie waited at the bottom of their drive with Beaver sitting in a lump by his feet. "Hello. I love expeditions, don't you?" He opened his knapsack so she could see the flashlight, Swiss Army knife, two bars of Cadbury's chocolate, and some sugarless gum.

"The gum cancels out the sugar in the chocolate." He offered her half of one bar.

"Thanks." Munching companionably, they walked down the hill, past the cemetery, past the church with the gold steeple and the stopped clock.

Ernie pointed. "Did you notice? No one else seems to have noticed. I think grown-ups don't look enough."

"I know the clock is stopped—I saw that when we moved here."

"Yes, but now it's at five o'clock and it was at three o'clock a few days ago."

"So it was. And?"

"It's all part of it." Ernie started up the stone steps to the library. "I think the witch cares about big things *and* little things."

"Like mice with their heads cut off," Rosemary whispered.

"What?"

"Three mice—no heads—on our front step this morning."

Ernie paused and scratched his nose. "Maybe. But cats do that anyway."

They climbed to the top step, where Ernie tied Beaver to the handrail. Rosemary pushed open the heavy wooden door with the bunch of dried wheat hanging from it. Inside was a high desk with a round woman behind it.

"Hello, Ernie. Hello." She smiled at Rosemary.

"This is Rosemary Morgenthau," Ernie said. "She lives in the white house at the top of the hill, next to us."

"I know," the librarian said. "And I'm glad to see you. Would you like to be part of our summer reading program? We have all sorts of prizes and charts to show how much you've read." She pointed to something that looked like a giant red thermometer on the wall.

Rosemary shook her head. "No, I can see you're not interested," the librarian said. "Just what *are* you interested in?" She came out from behind the desk, and Rosemary was reassured. She was an Ernie sort of person. Short and round and comfy.

"I want to find out something about the family who lived in our house long ago. Especially about the little girl who lived in my room."

Ernie nudged her.

"Or a little girl I *think* lived in my room."

"How long ago do you think this was, Rosemary? You see, the volumes are all by decades."

"Oh." Rosemary thought for a moment and guessed. "Maybe the 1840's? I think Dad said the house was built around then."

"Well, all the town histories are down in the basement, so follow me. But be careful on the steps, please!"

They followed her down a set of rickety stairs to a dark cellar with tiny cobwebbed windows.

"Let me see." The librarian reached up to the top shelf and took down an old green volume that had "Woodhaven, 1840–1850" printed on its spine. "Let's take this up to the light."

Back in the main room, Ernie and Rosemary sat side by side at the table and leafed through the book. The librarian went back behind her desk and folded new plastic covers around books.

"You could look at the names in the back," the woman said. "Try Otis. I think the family that originally built your house was named Otis. And there was another house just like it next door, built by his brother. But it burned down in the last century."

Ernie started.

Rosemary whispered, "We don't know if the witch was alive then. Besides, we're here to find out about my girl on the wallpaper, not the witch. If it is a witch," she added.

"Here, here's Otis," Ernie said. He turned to page 79.

"There it is!" Rosemary pointed.

Halfway down the page was Richard Otis's name in black print. Ernie's stubby finger followed the printing. "Richard Otis, married at thirty-two, had one child of Amanda Beals, who died at the age of twenty-five. The child was called Mathilda." Ernie's finger stopped and Rosemary leaned forward.

"Mathilda," she repeated.

"The father lost his house to his creditors in 1880 and Mathilda Otis left town and was never heard from again."

"Never found her." Rosemary breathed through her nose. "She just disappeared."

"How sad. That poor girl," Ernie said.

Rosemary turned the page. "There!"

The picture of her house was clear and sharp. In front of the house stood a thin, unpleasant-looking man with a drooping face. A small, pale woman stood beside him with a little girl pressed close to her skirts.

"Oh!" Rosemary gasped. It *was* her. The little girl on the wallpaper. The same corkscrew curls, the same pinched, unhappy face, the same dress, buttons marching up the thin chest to her chin.

Her throat squeezed in and Rosemary blinked, rapidly. She wouldn't cry in front of Ernie, in front of the librarian.

"Poor girl," Ernie was saying. "What a sad-looking little family. Is this the girl on your wallpaper, Rosemary?"

"Yes, yes it is." She began to cry after all, tears running down into her mouth. She felt something so dark and hopeless inside that it threatened to rise up and overwhelm her. She saw that same stick-figured child sitting alone, in her room. She heard harsh voices downstairs. She heard the sound of bottles smashing. A dark wind blew through her and with it, the sound of water dripping and wings rustling. Something black and fierce and vengeful rose in her, making her leap to her feet.

"Rosemary!" Ernie peered anxiously into her face. "Are you all right? What's wrong?" He shook her shoulder.

The sound of dripping water faded. The cold aching in her limbs drained away. The fierce anger seeped out, and all Rosemary could do was shake her head and cry.

"Are you all right, Rosemary?" The librarian stood by her. "Would you like me to call your mother? She could come pick you up."

"No." Rosemary wiped her eyes on Ernie's sleeve. "No, don't do that." I couldn't explain anyway, she thought. What could I say?

Ernie led her out the door, untied Beaver, and held her arm down the steps. She felt the soft warmth of his cushiony arm. She saw his blue eyes fixed on her as Beaver snuffled at her feet and made noises in his throat.

"It's okay," she said. "Okay. I can't explain, Ernie. Don't ask."

"Okay." He continued to hold her arm as they headed back up the hill. "But whatever it was that you saw back there, I bet it's all part of it, Rosemary. I just wish I knew what it means."

"So do I," she said softly, "so do I."

Chapter 13

She woke from a restless sleep. A sleep where sweet-smelling children invaded her woods, walked through her door, and sat on her sofa. A dream where a little girl took Emily onto her lap. *Her* lap.

Mathilda leaped out of bed and groaned as she hit the floor too hard. She fried up some pinecones over the hibachi and munched on them, offering a few tender pieces to Emily, who never opened her heart mouth.

Rosemary woke from a nightmare, sweating. A house on fire. A child who was so lonely her body ached. A house full of cold and silence. She pushed back her hair and pulled the blankets tight around her. Outside, the first birds sang in the linden tree. The darkness through the trees faded, as a layer of yellow started, bringing a piece of green, then a brilliant red. What was she going to do?

It was more serious than she had thought, sadder than she had imagined. And the worst of it was that if she didn't do something *soon*, she was afraid Mother and Dad would want to leave their beautiful house. For a house that was warm and dry.

Rosemary padded out to the phone in the hall and pressed the buttons. It rang six times before he answered.

"Ernie?" she whispered into the mouthpiece.

"It's early, Rosemary. Only five-thirty. Even Beaver's still asleep."

"I know, but we have to do something, Ernie. I'm afraid my family will want to leave if we don't do something about the—witch." Her tongue stumbled over the words.

Ernie breathed, "Mmmmmmm." Rosemary heard him scratching his head. "Okay, I'm coming over. Let's meet outside your house. Pack some food and we'll figure something out."

"Okay," she whispered, and set down the receiver. She ran to her room, pulled on jeans and a shirt, and went down to the kitchen. She packed Ritz Bits in a bag, some apples, and two juice packs. When she sat on the steps, the black cat came and curled around her leg, purring. "Shoo," she said, "go away. Go see Nicky, he likes you, shoo." But

111

perversely, the cat continued to purr and curl around her, thrusting its head against her hand. Rosemary jumped up and ran across the driveway, looking for Ernie.

Sunlight streamed into the cabin. It lit on Mathilda's seamed yellow face. It warmed the aged cheeks of Emily. It shone on the worn rag rug and the splintered floorboards. Something about it twitched at Mathilda.

Light, like a rug. Warmth, like a blanket. She put her face into the sunlight and turned it slowly back and forth. A sigh escaped her. Light in the morning. Light in her hair, which had once been some other color—something not as dark. Light on the cat that once had been hers. Mathilda held her hands out to the shaft of sun coming through the window. Slowly, slowly, she turned her hands back and forth, and for one second, the claws at the ends of her fingers seemed to shrink.

Ernie held out a chocolate bar and they shared it.

Rosemary crunched on the nuts. "I love chocolate first thing in the morning."

"Mmmm." Ernie's cheek bulged. "And last thing at night. And in the middle of the day. And for elevenses and three-sies, and in between times when the body is hungry and the spirit faint."

Rosemary smiled. She felt a rush of affection for Ernie—

112

his roundness, his hunger, the comfort of someone who watched The Three Stooges and didn't care about fossils or history or perfect bodies.

Ernie turned toward their woods and nodded. "That's where she is. You're right that it's time we did something."

"What can we do, Ernie?" Rosemary stood on one foot.

"Ask the witch what she wants."

Rosemary opened her mouth. "*Talk* to her?"

"Of course." Ernie patted Beaver, who slumped like a lost suitcase in a bus station. "That's the reasonable thing to do."

Rosemary shifted her weight to the other foot, pulled on her hair, and took a deep breath. "But . . ." Words escaped her again.

"But what, Rosemary?" Ernie said.

"But I'm afraid," she whispered.

"I know." He patted her hand. "I am too, but how will we ever find out what to do if we don't talk with her?" Ernie rubbed Beaver's back.

Mathilda jerked her head up. Something. Small feet. A clean child smell. And something else—fat as a suitcase and worn at the edges. It sniffed and sniffed and howled. Dog!

She hated dogs. They were too round and cozy. They were unbearably friendly and insincere. They put a head in your lap and ran off to put it in someone else's lap.

113

"Emily," Mathilda croaked, "they're in *our* woods."

So long, so long to find a place where no one bothered her. Where her smell was the only smell there. And now they—they were coming, invading, cutting open her quiet, dark wedge of the world. She opened her mouth and began to sing. From the back of her ancient throat, from the dried, withered mouth came a yowling and a screeching. Her hair stood on end as she sang, the trees began to shake outside, and owls bolted from sleep.

Ernie turned toward the woods and set off. Beaver was in front, sniffing and wagging his way down the grassy path. A crow flew overhead. The light grew and widened and suddenly sunlight blazed through the field. Birds called to each other, then stopped. Rosemary watched Ernie disappearing across her field and then pelted after him. How would she ever get to be a Rosemary instead of a Rosie unless she did something? Just as she was catching up to Ernie, a high, scratchy sound brought her to a halt.

Ernie stopped and looked at her. The sound pierced their ears, and they could not move. It was like a truck crashing to a stop, with the screech of brakes and the sound of splintering glass.

The sound went on and on until they dropped to the ground with their hands over their ears. Beaver sat in one place and howled, hair rising in a stiff ridge along his back.

"Oooh." Ernie sat back on his heels. "It's over." His face was pale as winter sun. "Maybe we should come back another day." He did not look at Rosemary.

Rosemary thought of Mother with her headache and sore legs; of Dad's books; of what it would be like to leave her room with the windows that divided up the trees and the sky. She took a deep breath, got up from the ground, and headed toward the woods.

After a short pause, Ernie whispered to Beaver, "Come on!" and followed.

At the edge of the woods hung a tangle of vines. They pushed through, with Beaver at their heels.

A dark shape flashed over them, once, twice. Ernie ducked and Beaver whimpered.

"Only an owl," Ernie said unsteadily. "Hunting."

"In the daylight?" Rosemary said.

"Come on." Ernie went forward. "We have to ask her what she wants. We have to find out why she's here."

Down the path they went, and suddenly Rosemary knelt and touched the damp earth. "Tracks," she whispered. "My bike, Ernie."

"Of course," he said. "I told you." He continued on to the stream. By the bank he stopped and pointed. Large sneaker tracks were imprinted in the mud, trailing off up the rise to a dark, rotting cabin.

For one long minute, everything was quiet. Rosemary

felt as if she'd been rushing through space and suddenly had come to rest on a foreign planet where all the rules of gravity were different. She might slide up into the sky. Ernie could grow antelope horns and gallop off into the woods.

Then the noise began. A chittering in the leaves, like thousands of tiny, devouring insects. The trees began to vibrate, the trunks shimmering in the light. The branches clicked overhead and the leaves at their feet whirled up their legs, blinding them. Crows flew over them so low their feet caught in Rosemary's hair.

Rosemary screamed and Beaver howled, turned tail, and they ran back down the path. Ernie stayed for a second longer, watching. Something yellow. Something shriveled and old as a mummy peered through that cracked window.

He cupped his mouth and shouted, "Oh wondrous aged one, what do you want?"

The branches clattered and leaves flew past his ears, bringing with them a terrible rotting smell.

"Want?" the voice shrieked. "Want?" Then the glass blew, the cabin roof lifted, and something dark and vast and shadowy hung over him. Ernie screamed and ran back down the path, out through the tangle of vines, across the field in great jumps, into the Morgenthaus' kitchen, where he slammed the door shut and locked it.

Rosemary shivered by the table while Beaver lay in a shapeless mass beneath, whimpering. Ernie opened his mouth.

116

"She—"

Rosemary shivered uncontrollably.

"She—"

Beaver lifted his head.

"She—"

Rosemary rushed to the sink and was sick.

Mathilda's Revenge

She settled to the ground and strode through the door. Mathilda swiveled her head from side to side. Nothing here. They hadn't got to the cabin. She'd made sure of that!

Her hair roiled behind her and she raced around the room, hissing. "My room! My cabin. My woods!"

She clamped her hands to her middle. She felt sick. That smell. *Their* smell. Clean-child sweat, laundry detergent, and a kind of flowery perfume. And the dog. He smelled of fur and warm fires and heated rooms.

Mathilda spat and a hole burned in the floor. The smell was an invasion, just as their being in *her* woods was an invasion. "Something," she hissed. "We need something to keep them from ever coming here again, Emily." If they came here, maybe they would steal Emily and throw her under a rock—the way those other children had so long ago. Mathilda clutched her chest and moaned.

Moths fluttered against the walls, black winged, brown winged, green winged. And one large wary toad regarded her with golden eyes.

She drummed her aching nails on the windowsill. Bad smells. Cold fog. Things stolen, a playground destroyed, children frightened. Pitiful. "I can do better, Emily, really I can." She was sure now that she had the power. Wasn't it her birthday in a few days' time? She rummaged in her brain for the date; "July sixth, or was it July seventh, Emily? Maybe I'll get a—present!" She seized on the word and patted the doll.

Emily. Now she would pay them back for abandoning the doll by the stream. Sitting back on her heels, she remembered.

Mrs. Pierce. With a bosom like a shelf trussed in butcher paper and hands like a fat, shiny doll's. "Mathilda!" she had screamed. "Mathilda! Stand up straight. Pull your stomach in. Keep your chin up! Up! Learn your letters. Spell by lamplight. Sew and sew and sew, and maybe someday some poor man will make you his wife, *which* I very much doubt, by the way!" And the class had roared with laughter, open red mouths, little hooting sounds rising up out of those red mouths fringed with spiky little teeth.

Mathilda ground her nails into the windowsill and it

crumbled beneath them. The sounds rising up, the laughter, out of it came her desire, like something dark and long, a long, dark rope pulled up from her insides, out through her mouth, out through the window. "My own!" she shrieked soundlessly. "Come to me! I need you!"

And from the mud by roadsides, from the dank mud in road ditches, from the ill-smelling swamps, they came—lurching, jumping, a living, slithering carpet.

Chapter 14

Rosemary sat with her legs curled under her on the bed. Freddy was on her lap, and from time to time she pressed her nose into the top of his fur. His smell calmed her heart and breathing. Her stomach still hurt. That walk down the tangled path. The horrible smell on the wind. The sound of the witch's voice that seared her ears and made her hair rise. The witch was stronger than they knew and more awful than they had imagined.

Rosemary almost burst into tears. What did she want? Did she hate them? What had they ever done to hurt her? What if they had to leave?

Only last night Dad had complained about his library, again. "Marjorie, if this weather keeps up, it could hurt my books, even with that machine going." He'd shaken a volume at them, as if it were their fault the weather was damp and cold and smelly.

"Your books, George," Mother said angrily. "What about my legs and my dancing? Just look at these joints!" And she'd thrust a swollen knee in front of them all, saying, "How can I teach like this? Answer me that!" And no one had answered.

Even Nicholas, who usually was so calm and ordered, had just complained to her. Leaning against her doorway, he'd said, "I've been thinking. You're right, there is something wrong with this house. Of course, it can't be a witch, but maybe the house is built over some ancient fossil bed with pockets of gas in it or something." He'd looked at her, hoping for agreement.

She'd watched him as if from very far away. He was just beginning to catch the edge of it, whereas she was right in the middle of it—a sea of blackness and hurt and fear where he couldn't reach her anymore. All she could say was, "Maybe you're right, Nicholas." He'd gone back to his room while she stayed on her bed, hoping for comfort, hoping for it all to go away.

Then something nudged at her, a sound through the window. She ran to it and opened it wider.

"Rose-mar-ee! Rose-mar-eeee!" It was Ernie! Rosemary pressed her nose against the screen but could see nothing. Just a black, inky sky with no stars and no moon.

122

"Rose-mar-eee, help!"

"Coming," she shouted through the screen. "I'm coming, Ernie."

The black cat brushed against her legs and Rosemary started. "You! Get away, shoo!" The cat arched its back, yawned, and prowled out of the room.

Rosemary grabbed her knapsack and thrust in her Boy Scout knife, flashlight, and a roll of tape. Dad always said duct tape took care of most of the world's ills, so she used it. She pulled on the knapsack and ran downstairs.

"Just going out for a little walk, Dad, back soon," she called out.

"Mmmmm," he answered from the library. In one jump, Rosemary was down the steps and racing across the lawn, down the ditch, up and onto the road. Her feet slid to one side and she fell.

"Ouch! *Oooooh!*" She pushed her hands down against something wet and cold and slimy. Rosemary jumped to her feet and got out the flashlight, shining its beam on the road. On what once was a road. Jumping, leaping, they went past, and went past, and went past. She began to shake and could not stop. Toads! With warty eyes and bumps all up and down their backs and sticky feet.

"Ernie!" she screamed.

His cry seemed nearer. "Rose-mar-eee! I'm up the road."

Beaver howled, a sound that sent goose bumps skittering up her back. A chill wind blew, lifting the hair from her neck. Something seemed to breathe behind her and Rosemary stumbled forward. Her stomach squeezed in and she swung the flashlight in a wide arch. Nothing there—except the flowing river of toads.

"Rosemary, I'm coming!"

Rosemary stood, one foot lifted. If Ernie could walk, then she would have to. At least try. How would she ever become a Rosemary instead of a Rosie if she didn't try?

She lifted her other foot and put it down. "Ooogh!" It slid off to the side. Another step, and the act of moving forward made something warm and dark and spicy flow down the back of Rosemary's throat, warming her stomach.

"Rosemary, be careful!" came Ernie's voice, closer now.

The warm spicy feeling flowed down her legs, and Rosemary went faster now, pushing forward. Think of Dad's hot soup in a red can stirred with a wooden spoon. Think of Nicholas bent over his fossils, holding an ancient fern to the light. Her foot slid to the side. Think of Mother's special rocking chair, warm by the fire.

"Rosemary!" She saw Ernie now, a darker patch of blackness with a small spot at its foot.

Rosemary took one last great step, arching up over the toads, and hooked her arm through Ernie's. He felt soft and comforting. Beaver groaned and leaned against her leg. Ernie just said, "Rosemary!"

"My house," she got out, and pulled on his arm. They waded back down the road, sliding as they went. Shoulder to shoulder, wind pushing their backs, they went across the ditch and stepped on Rosemary's lawn. There were fewer toads there. Across the dark space the porch glowed invitingly.

"Oh, porch!" Ernie sighed.

"My house," Rosemary cried. They stretched, reaching for the light. But it was as far away as ever.

Rosemary smelled hot soup and bread baking. She thought she heard a lullaby crooned on the wind, and the light lay like a warm, yellow blanket on the grass.

"Rosemary, we're not"—Ernie tugged at her arm—"not getting any closer." Legs lifted, they surged forward, but came no closer to the porch, its light and safety.

Rosemary tightened her grip on Ernie's arm. She felt such a tearing yearning for home that she almost fell.

"My house," she cried, "my door."

"My nothing," came a harsh voice at her back. "Not yours, *mine!*"

And for one second, Rosemary saw a face inside—small, wizened, and unhappy.

Ernie turned to Rosemary, his face a sharp white. They pressed forward together. The porch steps stayed just out of reach.

"Mine," came the gravelly, ancient voice. "Yours to leave. Yours to leave for *me!*" The voice rose in a shriek, the wind blasted them, and suddenly, they put their feet on the stone steps and pulled themselves through the porch door. Beaver slithered to a heap on the floor.

125

Rosemary looked and breathed in. Mother's feet still beat out a tempo on the floor above. Dad hummed to himself from the library, and she could hear the chink of Nicholas's fossils. The cat looked at them, its yellow eyes glowing.

"Home," she whispered.

"Home." Ernie sat on the floor, burying his face in Beaver's coat. Then he looked up. "Now we know what she wants, Rosemary. Your house."

Rosemary shivered. The safe sounds of the house flowed about them, and somehow, that made it worse. She began to sob with dry, raspy sounds.

"It's all right." Ernie got up and hugged her. "It's just words, she can't hurt us, the cat can't hurt us. I think," he added.

It's not just words, Rosemary wanted to shout, but she was trembling and crying too hard. It was the wanting inside the dark and the fierce yearning for that lit doorway that undid her, for now she knew how the witch felt.

Mathilda Visits

Mathilda wished that the girl weren't so little. She could feel her curled up inside the house, shivering, with the dog and the boy beside her. Mathilda wished the girl's hair didn't remind her of hers, that her quiet voice didn't make her remember how invisible she used to feel.

The witch flew past the second-story window and looked in, pressing her nose against the glass. Different now. With a great big canopy bed with dolls propped on it in rows. She had so much.

Mathilda bundled herself onto a branch of the linden tree. It was a towering tree covered with rustling leaves. Sounds came from below. Someone ran downstairs. There were exclamations and cries.

"Toads! Come look, Mom!" That was the brother.

"Toads, oh, no!" The mother stuck her head through the porch door and stayed there, frozen. The father and the boy stood together on the porch steps, watching and rocking on their heels.

He was so different from her father. This one was tall and softly rounded. He put his arm around the boy and left it there, as they talked together. Had Father *ever* once put his arm around her?

And there—there was the mother, now hurrying to be with them. Her footsteps were small and light as a moth fluttering. Mother's footsteps had been soft and quick, too.

Laughter floated up to the tree. It hurt her insides. The man's arm around the boy made her chest ache. The mother's red hair glowing in the porch light drew her throat in.

Family. Together.

Mathilda fidgeted on the tree branch. Something rose inside that made her want to ride screaming to the highest cloud. She hissed at the cat that stood on the porch, its golden eyes glowing. The cat turned and looked at her, and then went up to the father and deliberately scratched his ankle.

The man jumped into the air. "*Oooh*, you little beast!" He peered at the animal in a bewildered way.

"What happened?" the mother said.

"That cat just scratched me. Deliberately!"

"Hush," the mother said. "You must be mistaken."

"No, he wouldn't do that," the boy said.

"I'm not so sure," the father answered. "I'm remembering now what Rosemary said."

The witch hummed to herself. They looked up for an instant, not seeing her, but hearing the gravelly rattle of her voice.

"What's that?" The boy's voice wavered.

"Wind in the leaves," the father said firmly.

The woman shivered and put her arms around her husband and son. "I don't like this. I don't like this at all!"

Mathilda rose noiselessly into the air and surveyed the river of toads below, moving, lurching, jumping. It stilled the ache inside. It soothed the hurt behind her eyes. Toads. Hers. Ugly and scary. She could feel the fear rising from the porch, a sweetly rotten smell. That was good. Mathilda flew back to the woods and settled onto her couch, pulling Emily onto her lap. Now they would stay away from her cabin. Now she would get what she wanted. At last.

Toads Come to Woodhaven

Johnny peered through the windshield. It wasn't exactly foggy, but it wasn't exactly clear either. There was something brown up ahead. He pushed up the brim of his hat. "Got to get my eyes checked," he muttered to himself.

Suddenly, his front tires began to slide. He gripped the wheel tighter and pumped the brakes softly. Once—twice. Let up on the brakes—once—twice.

The big rig slid to the side, came out of the skid, and then skidded again.

"Christmas!" Johnny exclaimed, as the rig swung slowly sideways and surged across the road. He saw trees spinning by, branches scraped his truck, something shrieked and groaned, and the truck came to a halt.

He let out his breath and felt his chest. Everything was okay. No harm done. But the truck? He rolled down the window and looked out. He was perched on the edge of a ditch, held back by a thick knot of trees.

"Thank God for those!" He saw the road off to his left, but it didn't look like a road. It was moving, and it was brown. The rest of the cars on the highway had come to a dead halt. Some had skidded off to the side, as he had, and the rest just stayed on the road with motors running and lights on. People didn't get out of their cars but rolled down their windows and shouted to each other.

"Can you believe this?"

"What *is* it? What *are* they?"

A child began to cry somewhere, long wails rising up. The skin prickled on Johnny's neck.

"What's going on?" a man called through his window.

"Frogs. That's what's going on!" Johnny said quietly. "Frogs. And I don't like it neither!"

In Mrs. Nan's restaurant, people gathered around the counter and yelled at the same time.

"Frogs . . . creeping, crawling. . . ."

"Toads! Gotta be toads!"

"Hate them things!"

"My car all squished—"

"I slid off the road and you should see . . ."

"Quiet!" Mrs. Nan shouted. "Quiet down!"

"Now hush, take a seat and we'll talk this all out." Mrs. Nan pushed her hair back from her face and poured out coffee for everyone within reach. "I don't remember John Quill saying anything about frogs or toads. Tell me, one at a time."

And so, one at a time, they told Mrs. Nan about the frogs, or toads. How the road had looked the same as usual one minute, and the next thing they knew, it was covered with these things and their cars skidded on them.

"Horrible," Mrs. Nan said with fascination, coffeepot suspended in one hand. "Horrible!" Because she lived over the restaurant, she had not been out to walk or drive and so had missed the toads.

"Chemicals!" said a bald man in a denim jacket. "Probably some kind of waste dump nearby and everything's out of control. You can't fool Mother Nature, you know!" He bit his thumb.

"Chemicals, phooey!" said a woman in high heels. "It's just plain, ugly, disgusting frogs. Probably too hot a summer or something. Or cold," she added confusedly. "Actually, it's been cold."

"Yeah, greenhouse effect," murmured a man in a running suit.

"Well." Mrs. Nan set down the coffeepot. "Whatever it

is, whoever they are, we don't want them—that's what!"

"Hear, hear," the regulars said.

And Mrs. Nan switched on the TV over the counter, spinning the dial, hoping to catch a forecast by John Quill that would explain a world gone haywire.

Chapter 15

Dad's footsteps thumped below. Mother's steps were quick and light as a moth fluttering against a wall. Water ran. Dad coughed.

Everything sounded normal. But it wasn't. Rosemary sighed and hugged Freddy. They'd had a whole day to get used to the toads, after last night: the night the witch blasted them with her breath; the night she finally understood what the witch wanted.

"I don't know, George." Mother's voice was loud enough to come through the floorboards. "This place is getting to me. I don't know if I want to stay. I swear, I think there's a hex on the house!" The bedsprings creaked.

"Now, now, Marjorie, not a hex. We don't believe . . ." Dad's voice was softer, harder to hear.

"Oh, don't we?" Mother's voice rose. "What about the cold? You call that normal? And that awful fog that lasted a whole week? And that mold on your books, and my aching legs? I feel like an eighty-year-old woman, George!"

"I know it's been hard, Marjorie, but it'll get—"

"Better my foot! Rosemary's bike is gone, just vanished into thin air. You know how things like that upset me. It doesn't feel safe, George. All those things lost from the shed—moving doesn't account for them all—and now this."

There was a hush. Then Rosemary heard one word, almost whispered. "Toads."

"There are a lot. Quite interesting really, Marjorie. When I went to get a paper at Bob's store this morning, they told me the toads are all over the town now. Cars slid off the road and the Audubon Society is investigating."

"Audubon Society! We don't need that. We need an exorcism, George!"

"Hush, hush, it's just been a bad start, Marjorie—"

Mother's voice cut in. "Do you know how much I *hate* toads?"

"Hush, it will be all right. I promise." The talking stopped and the house was quiet.

Rosemary clutched the top of her nightgown. That was it. Mother wanted to go. All their dreams of firefly watching from the porch, of picking Queen Anne's lace in the meadow, of having their own special rooms—gone. Just as it was getting to be hers. Just as she was beginning to know the sounds in the house and the names of the flowers outside and how the morning light lay on her bed. Just then.

Rosemary turned over and sighed. She kept hearing the cold, harsh voice of the witch screaming, "Not yours—mine!"

They all wanted this house—a home. Nicholas, Mother and Dad, the witch. And me. Something itched at Rosemary, made her fidget and turn over once again. She could see that small, unhappy face inside each time she closed her eyes.

Rosemary turned on the light and got out of bed, walking softly to the corner. She crouched down and put her finger on the wallpaper. "Oh, small person of long ago, what did you know? Did the witch take the house from you? Did—?"

Rosemary pushed back her hair and looked more closely at the picture. Those cheeks. That ragged, unfinished hair. That fierce, sad face.

"You! You! It was *your* house and now you want it back! Mathilda."

She shivered, grabbed Freddy, and jumped back into bed. That wizened face and cold, yearning voice pulled at her. So unhappy. So much wanting. Her eyes filled with tears, and she whispered to Freddy, "How did it happen?"

First there was the girl. She could see her clearly inside—a skinny body, a squeezed face, and a papa who also looked thin and morose. Will I turn into a witch? Rosemary started. Maybe it was something about this house, this room. You started out a little girl and somewhere along the way you turned into a witch. All that unhappiness, all that meanness—for Rosemary knew that was part of it, too—changed you. Into something black and dark that hovered overhead and terrified children—terrified her. What would Dad have to say about this? What category could explain this?

"A home," she said into Freddy's ear. "She has to have a home. But not this one." Maybe—maybe, if she could help the witch find a home, she would be happy and leave them alone.

What made a home and how could she bring it to the witch? Was home the sound of footsteps on the floorboards? Maybe it was the way light slanted through the window on a favorite rag rug, picking out the greens and reds. Or it could be the smell of coffee floating up the stairs and the sound of steam knocking in radiators on a cold morning.

Rosemary turned over and buried her nose in the pillow. Maybe it was smells. The smell of clean sheets, just off the line. The smell of fresh flowers on the living room table. Muffins baking in the morning. Someone who cared about rooms welcoming people.

Rosemary knew. It was coming down to breakfast in the morning and finding your place all set with orange juice poured into a glass and cornflakes on the table. It was the sound of Mother's feet thumping on the floor as she pirouetted in front of the mirror. It was Dad humming as he took a book out, flipped through it, and put it back on the shelf. It was the sound of Nicholas picking up his fossils and setting them down. It was the linden tree scratching her window in a gentle wind. It was red phlox in July and Queen Anne's lace in the meadow and fireflies in jars with maybe—just maybe—a ghost story at the very end.

Rosemary turned on her back and stared into the dark. How could she take any of those things to the witch? Finally, she fell asleep, still wondering.

Chapter 16

While the light slanted new across the floor, Rosemary climbed out of bed and pulled on jeans and a green shirt. She got out her knapsack and knelt. Her hands trembled. She was the only one who knew. She should call Ernie, but couldn't, somehow. Because she was the only one who knew about the unhappy face on the wall and the person that girl had become, Rosemary had to do this on her own. It was all part of finding a name for herself, something she could hold on to. Rosemary—finder of names and unhappy persons of long ago.

"Home," she whispered to Freddy, propped beside her on the floor. "Let's start with Maude." Rosemary plucked the white ceramic cat from the bookcase and put it into the knapsack. Maude would keep the witch company on long, lonely nights.

Food. The witch's voice had been harsh and gravelly. Maybe she needed some chocolate to fill and sweeten her. Rosemary thrust a whole bar of Cadbury's fruit and nut chocolate into the sack. Warmth. She stood and rubbed her arms. How about that white sweater with the red stripes that was too big for her? Perfect for the witch.

"Something to fill her mind," Rosemary said to Freddy. She took her favorite book off the shelf, *The Long Winter* by Laura Ingalls Wilder. It was all about survival and bravery and winning through in the end to spring when the ice melted and friends came by to celebrate. Maybe the witch had nothing to cheer her during the cold, windy evenings.

She had a sudden image of that dark, terrifying thing alone in the dark. How could she go and talk to her? All alone?

But she wouldn't go alone. She thrust Freddy into the sack and rubbed his ears. All these years he had made her brave, helped her past strangers with large eyes and too-big dogs.

Rosemary crept down the stairs and paused by the kitchen door. They would be worried if they woke and found her gone. She scribbled on a scrap of paper, "Gone for a walk, back soon, Rosemary. 5:30 A.M."

There. Out the door and across the lawn. She paused. The toads were gone—gone as if they had never been! Her knees wobbled and her stomach ached. She looked back at the house. The early light slanted against the white clapboards. The faded shutters were soft and muted as old moss. The windows held blue sky and wispy clouds. The wicker chairs on the porch waited for people to sit in them.

Rosemary gripped the shoulder straps of her knapsack and walked down the path to the woods. The flowers drooped by the path, as if an early frost had bit them. This. This was what she was going to see. A creature that sent out cold and made things die. That sent toads and fog. Rosemary almost felt the bones in her chest trembling and sucked in a breath. If she didn't go—if she couldn't convince the witch to go—*they* would have to leave. And go back to Garden City.

Rosemary walked to the edge of the woods and paused. A thick tangle of vines hung down. She pushed with a shoulder, a vine caught around her neck, and she pulled it off, trembling.

She folded her arms across her chest and gripped them, hard. Something caught at her feet, and Rosemary stumbled, almost falling on a hidden rock.

She thought of the porch, waiting. Of Mother twirling in the blue room. Of Dad humming in his library. Of Nicholas staring happily at a handful of dirt. She was here because of them.

On through the periwinkle that plucked at her feet, on to the stream just ahead. A can with a piece of baling twine rested on a stone. Rosemary caught her breath. It looked so ordinary.

Stepping carefully on the wet stones, Rosemary hesitated at the bank. It seemed a marker, a boundary. Reluctantly, she put one foot on the muddy bank. Then another. Up the rise. Her feet dragged and the air felt heavy and brown. The cabin was just ahead, dark and moldy in the dense shadows of two pines. No sun touched its windows. The doorway gaped like a black mouth. Just beside it leaned her bike.

Rosemary stopped. She couldn't. Not go in there. Not see *her*. Maybe Garden City wasn't so bad after all. Then she thought of her room with the rose wallpaper and the window that divided up the trees and the sky. *Hers*. Rosemary breathed in, clenched her teeth, and went up to the doorway. There was a faded rag rug on the floor and a poster on the wall. An embroidered pillow rested on the couch, and something long and dark and shapeless lay there. Its hair spread over it like a black thicket.

Rosemary turned to run, but a sound stopped her. The creature was snoring.

Just as the safe, human sound began to quiet her fears, the smell and the dense air of the cabin gathered and assaulted her nose. Something old and ancient as a forgotten seabed. Something dead as an animal left on the road in the sun.

Rosemary sneezed, and the thing shot off the couch,

142

gathering itself in the corner. Pieces of clothing flew about it. The hair rose straight up and settled, slowly. The eyes burned yellow.

"So—you've come."

Chapter 17

Rosemary could not move. The witch's breath blasted her, and she choked. The witch's hair rose and fell, rose and fell, and her eyes dimmed a little.

"Better come in." An arm gestured toward the sofa. "But don't sit on my doll!" she shrieked.

Rosemary crept to the sofa and sat, hunched forward. She gathered herself together with her arms, as if she were a loose bundle of clothing that might fall apart at any moment. Rosemary took deep, long breaths, and her heart slowed—for a moment.

The witch stood in the corner, clothes still roiling about her with a sound like a far sea hissing.

"I," Rosemary began, then stopped. The air felt thick and brown—impossible to breathe. "I brought you—some things." She pulled off the knapsack and opened it.

Rosemary's hands trembled so that she almost dropped the red-and-white-striped sweater. "For you." She held it out. "To keep you warm."

The witch shot out a bony hand, and the sweater leaped to her, settling around the hunched shoulders.

Rosemary drew out the book and offered it.

"What?" The witch's arms rose and fell, and the lines on her face slid sideways.

"A book!" Rosemary gasped. She wanted to cry, but she was too scared. The air clotted in her throat and she coughed again. "A book, to read at night. For company. It's my favorite," she gabbled, "about the long winter when Laura and her family almost starve. . . ."

"Quiet!" hissed the witch, grabbing the book. She thrust it inside the sweater. "What do you know of starving?" She spat and a hole burned open by Rosemary's foot. Rosemary pulled her foot back quickly and wrapped her arms around her chest again. But it did not help. She put her hand inside the sack and stroked Freddy's nose. Her breathing slowed.

The witch leaned forward. "What else? Presents. That's the word—presents. It's my birthday. You remembered!" For a moment, the lines disappeared on her face, and the hair settled on the witch's shoulders. Rosemary saw an old, haggard woman with the slip of a girl looking out through wide, scared eyes. She thought of the picture on her wallpaper and felt braver.

"Yes." Rosemary seized on the word. "A birthday. I thought—I thought you might need a birthday, a celebration." Suddenly she felt so sorry for the witch that she almost cried. Never a birthday. Never a cake. Never anyone to remember who you were and how wonderful it was when you were born.

The witch came and sat by Rosemary. Rosemary shrank against the sofa back and closed her eyes.

"A celebration," the witch sighed, and Rosemary coughed. The witch's breath was ancient and sad, like the last banana turning black in a fruit bowl.

"I imagine you are very old," Rosemary whispered. Her hands jumped convulsively, and she put one on top of the other. She opened her eyes but did not look sideways.

"Oh, yes." The witch took up a faded rag doll with purple hearts for eyes and a mouth. "I am quite, quite old. I've seen summers come and go. Winters come and go, more than I can tell. How the ice gets in my bones. But all the ones I knew are gone!" She jumped to her feet and laughed, a harsh, grating sound. "Gone, and I am left—*me!*" She thumped her chest. "Mathilda!"

"Mathilda," Rosemary said softly. "Happy birthday, Mathilda. Here's some birthday chocolate."

The witch seized it and stuffed it into her mouth, wrapper

and all. The room filled with the sound of crunching and sighing. "Cho-co-late?" she repeated.

"Chocolate," Rosemary said. "Candy, something sweet."

"Sweet," the voice faltered, "sweet. I never had this cho-co-late before. Father didn't believe in anything sweet."

Rosemary sighed and her shoulders dropped. The witch's eyes weren't so fierce now. The clothes had stopped moving. The hair lay in ragged drifts against her humped shoulders. She looked shrunken and pitiful. She looked like someone who needed a stuffed bear.

"Anything else?" Mathilda asked.

"Yes, a cat, a white cat to keep you company." Rosemary offered Maude on the palm of her hand.

The witch stepped forward and knelt. A long yellow finger with a black claw at its tip reached out. It touched the porcelain cat softly. It stroked the smooth back. It touched the blue ceramic eyes and fingered the pink ceramic bow.

"The best present," she sighed. "A cat, for company." The words jerked out. "Pretty. I had a cat, once. It went away."

Suddenly, Rosemary wondered if Dad would have a special category for witches. Something like Being Kind to Eccentrics, or perhaps How to Cope With Impossible People. Except that she's not a person, Rosemary thought, and there is no category that fits.

Her hand reached for the sack, then drew back. She couldn't. Just because Mathilda looked sad—just because Freddy might comfort the witch.

147

Mathilda sighed again. "Everyone went away." Then she stood. "What about Emily? Did you bring a present for Emily?"

Rosemary looked blankly at the witch, who held out the worn doll with the purple hair and shook it. "Emily needs a present, too. Everyone forgot her, too." The witch's eyes glowed yellow.

Rosemary trembled and reached inside her sack. Her fingers touched Freddy, the only thing left. The witch stared at her, eyes burning yellow, and Rosemary drew out the bear.

"Here." She held him out. "Here's my teddy bear, for Emily—and you." And for one moment, she didn't mind giving Freddy away. The lines wavered on the witch's face, and Rosemary clearly saw, as if looking at a rock coming into view under shifting water, the face of the girl on her wallpaper.

"Freddy will help you, and Emily. He's comforting." She felt such a yearning for Mathilda, to give her all the things she needed, to smooth the etched lines on her face and erase the sad, unhappy girl who lived inside. Rosemary reached out and touched Mathilda's hand.

Mathilda jumped and held her hand to the light. Slowly, she raised it to her nose and sniffed the skin where Rosemary had touched it.

"People," she moaned. "Soap. Fires. Warmth. I heard people laughing." She sat beside Rosemary and hugged

148

Freddy and Emily to her chest. The words jerked out: "Thank you—for my presents."

Now, Rosemary thought. Now is the time to say it. "I know you want a home, but this is not your home anymore. It's ours."

The witch rose and her hair flew about her. The eyes burned. "Not yours, mine!" she shrieked, and the roof lifted.

Rosemary pressed back against the couch. The words dried in her mouth. She couldn't go on, couldn't stay here. No matter if they had to go back to Garden City. No matter if they all had to leave their special rooms behind. Then she saw Freddy clutched in the witch's arms. He made her brave.

"No." She pushed the words out. "Not yours. Ours. These presents are for you to make a new home with—one of your own someplace else. A cat and a bear for company. A book for fun. Chocolate to feed you. A sweater to keep you warm."

Mathilda hovered over the couch, and Rosemary flattened herself. "A sweet—a cat—sweater," and suddenly, the witch settled to the floor and everything collapsed about her.

"Go! Out of my sight—girl with the raggedy hair. Get out!"

Rosemary ran through the door, jumped over the stream, and raced through the tangle of vines. Up the path, through the kitchen door—she stopped. The cat stalked past her, tail held high and eyes veiled. No glowing yellow stare; no puffed-out fur; no sly looks. Just a cat with dark fur and a chewed ear. Rosemary breathed out and said, "Good-bye, cat. Go back to wherever you came from."

The cat waved its tail imperiously, walked down the steps, turned right by the dogwood bush and disappeared. Rosemary closed the door and sighed. Now. She pelted up the stairs with only one thought—to get clean. She leaped into the shower fully clothed and turned the water on, hard. Soaping her arms and hair and taking deep breaths of the sweet, clean steam, Rosemary looked down. The water that ran out from her shirt and pants was brown.

Anything Can Happen

"They're gone." Johnny Preston sat with a bump on the high stool.

Mrs. Nan put her elbows on the counter and smiled. "I know. I listened to John Quill this morning and he gave us the news. He said it was a strange—" she paused and scratched her cheek—"a strange local phenomenon."

"All you had to do," Neil Baldwin said, lighting a cigarette, "was look out the window. Just look out the window and you'd of seen them things was all gone."

Mrs. Nan gave him a smug glance. "I did look out the window, but I like to hear it from John Quill first."

"John Quill, John Schmill," said one of the customers in a long baseball cap pulled low over his eyes. "What matters is them stinking creatures is gone. I hated them. My wife hated them. My little girl hated them. My dog hated them."

"But what do you think . . ." Johnny mused, taking a deep bite of his fresh doughnut.

"Made them come out?" Mrs. Nan finished for him. "We don't know. John Quill doesn't know. No one does. They just piled out of those swamps at the edge of town and swarmed over our lawns."

" 'Tain't natural," the man in the baseball cap said.

"There's a lot of stuff that 'tain't natural." Neil Baldwin laughed. "That cold fog we had for a week. That smell— like the dump was filled to the top with garbage."

"Well, that's because they let the old dump manager go—"

"Dump manager!" cried Mrs. Nan. "Call it by its name. Garbage man!"

"Let the old dump manager go," Johnny finished. "Silly nits. He was the best guy we've ever had—and nice, too."

"Niceness doesn't matter at the dump," said Mrs. Nan, neatly flipping Johnny's eggs.

"Sure it does," said Phil. "Niceness always matters." And they were off, delving into the history of the dump and all its ill-tempered managers over the years. The fierce, short man who yelled at everyone, as if it were their fault they brought trash to his dump. The tall, bony man who lay limply against the dumpsters, taking no interest in the people who came.

152

Johnny took a sip of coffee and pushed his hat back. He guessed it was all right. Everything seemed to be all right. But who knew? If cold fogs could come swirling out of the hills and legions of toads cover their roads, anything could happen, couldn't it?

Chapter 18

"They're gone!" Mother danced into the kitchen, a whirl of blue tights and purple leotard. "The toads are gone," she sang, pulling coffee out of the cupboard and filling the pot with water. "The cold fog is gone, I feel human again, I can dance again!" She leaped across the kitchen floor.

"What's gone?" Dad shambled into the kitchen, scratching his hair. He sat at the table and proceeded to rub his face, hard and methodically.

"The toads. My headache. The ache in my bones." Mother poured out the water and switched on the coffee maker. She put fresh muffins into the toaster oven and set raspberry jam on the table.

Dad peered out the window and mumbled, "Gone! Just

like that. I'm not awake yet." He beckoned to Marjorie, and she came and sat on his knee, burrowing into his shoulder. "Mmmmm," he said into her ear. "Mmmmmmmm. I am glad."

"I can move my toes again." Mother wiggled them and smiled. "I can move my wrists again." She waved them in the air.

Nicholas came into the kitchen and pulled out his favorite dusty cereal. "Did you see? The toads have disappeared. I wanted to look at them again and take some notes."

Dad smiled at him. "Notes. When the end of the world comes, you will be taking notes."

"What's wrong with that? And did anyone see my cat?"

"Why, no, Nicholas, isn't it upstairs somewhere?" Mother asked.

"I felt him leave this morning," he answered. "He was sleeping all curled up on my bed, and suddenly he leaped off and ran down the stairs. But I don't see how he could've gotten out." He went to the electric can opener and turned it on. "This usually brings him in."

But the promising whir brought no cat, no swish of the tail. Nicholas slumped at the table. "I was just getting to know that cat. I liked him."

"I was just beginning to not like him," Dad grumbled. "A bad-tempered piece of goods if ever I saw one. That scratch!" He pulled up his pants leg, showing a long red scar.

Rosemary stood just out of sight in the doorway. There it was. Just as she'd imagined it. Mother pouring out orange juice. Dad rubbing his face and talking in a muffled, sleepy voice. Nicholas talking and eating dusty cereal. Home.

She walked into the kitchen. "I didn't like that cat, Nicky, he was creepy."

"But all cats are creepy," Nicky protested. "It's their nature."

"It is not!" Rosemary sat. "Remember that cat we had once, Alfie? He was sweet and fat and just lay around purring. He was like a rug. This cat was sly and suspicious and—" She stopped as Dad stared at her, coffee cup suspended in midair.

"What's wrong, Dad?" Rosemary fidgeted with her still-wet hair. If only they knew. If only she could tell them—nothing was wrong, now. She hoped.

"Nothing's wrong"—he grinned—"and everything's right. I just like to hear you talk, that's all." He beamed at her. "Sly and suspicious. Nice words. I like the way you put them together."

"Oh, Dad!" Rosemary sipped her juice, embarrassed. She wished he could have heard her talking to the witch. *That* was talking—when you couldn't, when you had to, when the words were like hard stones in her mouth and her tongue had disappeared somewhere and her lips were dry as the badlands. Could she have done it without Freddy? She won-

156

dered if the witch was being nice to him. She felt a hollow ache thinking of her bed with no Freddy on it.

Mother raised a leg and wiggled her toes. "See that?"

"Toes, Mother, thirty-eight-year-old toes at that," Nicholas intoned. "Dredged up from a coniferous forest by the famous paleontologist Nicholas Gray Morgenthau! A promising young lad with a career ahead of him . . ."

Rosemary poked him, hard. "Stop showing off. Stop sounding like a book! Talk like a real person for a change!"

He looked at her, surprised. "This is real—this is me. Mom's toes work. I'm making a joke, get it? But maybe you're too—"

"Nicholas," Mother warned. "I won't have you two squabbling on this beautiful day. The sun is out. It is not cold. There is no fog. And the toads have disappeared!" She spread her arms wide and pirouetted.

Nicholas stood and went to the window. "Where did they go to, do you think?"

Dad stood beside him. "Back to the swamps, back to the ditches. Must have been some kind of phenomenon— overbreeding or the greenhouse effect."

"Ha!" Rosemary said, and bit into her muffin slathered with raspberry jam. Home. Orange juice and muffins and a little bit of an argument at the breakfast table with someone there to stop you before it got too nasty.

"Ha, what, Rosemary?" Dad said.

"Thank you for calling me Rosemary," she said. "Ha, greenhouse effect. Ha, overbreeding. That had nothing to do with it."

"What did then?" Nicholas asked sharply.

Rosemary bit her lips, hard. The words almost rushed out: "The witch, Mathilda, that lived in our woods. The witch that I think is going, or gone." But the words stayed just behind her teeth. It was enough that Dad had called her Rosemary. That he liked the way she talked. She didn't want anyone making fun of her for believing in witches.

"Something else," she said airily. "Something you don't know about."

"Hmmmph," Nicholas grumped. "Did you see my cat? Or let him out this morning?"

"Mmmm, I did. He ran past me when I came in this morning from my early walk. And I don't think, Nicky, that he's coming back." She pointed to the scrap of paper on the table. "See, I left a note for you."

"Five thirty A.M.," Mother exclaimed. "That's early. Didn't you sleep well, dear?"

"Of course I slept well! Under my own canopy in my own room with the windows that divide up the trees and the sky."

Dad set down his coffee cup and tears came to his eyes. "Rosemary, that is truly beautiful. Here." He jumped up and grabbed a piece of notepaper and a pencil. "I'm going to write this down. I think you are becoming a poet."

He scribbled, muttering, "Windows—divide up—trees and sky."

Rosemary turned the word over in her mouth. "A poet. Me, a poet." That was a name—just for her. Something like a small, thready song began inside and would not stop.

"You're a poet and you don't know it," Nicky sang and poked her, softly.

"Maybe I'll have to get a writing pad," she said, surprised. "And some pens. Maybe even a desk."

"I think so, Rosemary," Dad said. "Writers need those things."

"No they don't," Mother said. "That's not what makes a writer. Pens and paper and desks."

"What does, Mom?" Nicky asked.

"Trees. Clouds. The way the wind blows. The sound of a child crying and being comforted. Fires crackling in the fireplace with smoke that smells like apples. Leaf houses in the fall and sliding down the hill on your bottom, laughing. People getting older and losing their hair. Aching toes. Those make writers."

Dad took her on his knee again and wrapped his arms around her. "Now I know where Rosemary gets her poet genes. From you." He kissed her loudly and Rosemary looked at Nicholas, embarrassed. He raised his eyebrows and grinned.

The phone rang sharply and Rosemary jumped to answer it.

" 'Lo, Rosemary," came Ernie's voice.

" 'Lo," she said.

"I think she's gone—or going," Ernie said. "The air feels different. It smells like real air now. My mother sang a song this morning—on key!" He laughed and Rosemary heard Beaver whuffling in the background. "What did you do?"

"I went to see her," Rosemary whispered into the mouthpiece. But the noise from the kitchen was so raucous, nobody heard.

"All by yourself?"

"All by myself," she said proudly.

"Brave Rosemary. I'm coming over." He hung up the phone.

Five minutes later, a sweaty Ernie burst through the kitchen door. "Hello, Mrs. Morgenthau, Mr. Morgenthau, Nicholas." He shook hands with all of them.

"Are you still running for office?" Dad joked.

"Not yet." Ernie took a seat at the table, and Mother poured some juice for him.

Nicholas smiled at him. "I'll vote for you when you do."

Ernie grinned. "Maybe I'll run for mayor when I'm bigger. They shake hands a lot and get to go to lots of free dinners."

Rosemary wanted her arms to grow long enough to fold everyone inside them. She imagined them all sitting on the wicker chairs on the porch with something to keep them linked and connected.

"Mother?" she said.

"Mmmm?"

"What happened to those ghost stories you were going to tell on the porch with the Queen Anne's lace in the meadow and fireflies?"

Mother stood on her toes and her hair flew out. "You want to hear one? You're getting braver, Rosemary." She kissed the top of her head and pulled Rosemary after her.

The rest followed and they all sat in wicker chairs, which creaked and rustled.

"I think it's too early for Queen Anne's lace, but the fireflies will be out tonight." Mother pointed to the meadow, where pink flowers dotted the green grass. Swallows dipped overhead and a loud bee pushed against the porch gutter.

"Are you ready, Rosemary?" Mother asked as she folded her legs under her.

Rosemary looked at them all and wished so hard that her spine tingled. If only she could tell them—not just how brave she'd been, but what the witch was like. How sad. How small. How forgotten.

"I'm ready," she said, and smiled. "And do you know what? Let me tell it this time, Mom. I have a story I want to tell." She looked at Nicholas, willing him to understand what she was trying to do.

"Once there was a little girl who lived all alone in a big, white house. She wasn't actually *all* alone, but she felt all

161

alone. Everyone she loved had gone away and her father didn't really live there anymore."

"What do you mean, didn't really?" Nicholas began, and then stopped himself at a look from Rosemary. "Okay, go on."

"No one liked her in her town. Something awful happened to her, I'm not sure what, and she had to leave her house. That's when she decided to be a witch." Rosemary knew suddenly that that was so.

"A witch," breathed Nicholas, and Dad shifted in his chair.

The words spilled out of her mouth, as if they came from some secret place even she, Rosemary, could not name. "She learned how to call the night creatures to her. She learned about spells under a dark, thin moon, and special spells that made her lips tremble under the full, white moon. She learned how to call down sickness on cows and sheep and horses. She learned to steal things from people so that they worried about losing their minds."

Mother nudged Dad. "Like us," she whispered.

"But what she wanted most was a home. Her own home. To have it back, with a mother and a father and a cat and warm fires. And so—she set out to cast out the owners of the house and get her home back. She used spells, and witch language, weather, stealing, and cold."

She paused. No one spoke. Finally Dad looked at her.

162

"Is that all, Rosemary? What happened? Did it work? Did they leave?"

She smiled at him, but did not answer. Nicholas answered for her, with an intense look, drumming his fingers on the chair arm. "No, they didn't leave. And you know why?"

"Why?" asked Ernie, hugging his knees close.

"Because somebody very brave lived in that house who made the witch go away. Don't ask me how, but that's what she did."

"And where did the witch go, once she left?" Mother asked, worried. "Did she find a home of her own? Was she still wicked and mean?"

Rosemary took a deep breath. "I don't know that part. I know that she left. Maybe she went back to living in the wild. Maybe she flew off into the night to find her own star to live on. Maybe she turned into dark smoke that vanished in the night air."

Dad breathed out. "Beautiful. Where's my notebook?"

Rosemary looked at Ernie and he looked back. She felt tears in the corners of her eyes and saw Ernie blinking rapidly.

Suddenly Nicholas stood and shouted. "Hey, Rosemary—there's your bike, up against the wall, in the shadows. It must have been there all the time!"

Rosemary walked slowly over to her bike, Ernie beside her. They both touched the seat carefully, warily, as if something of Mathilda still clung to it. Rosemary felt the words choke in her throat.

Ernie sucked in a breath and pointed to the floor. Between the front wheel of the bike and the porch wall, two black eyes gleamed. Ernie bent, pulled something out, and held it toward Rosemary.

"Look. Look what she left you."

And, as if the words swung by on a cold, gray wind, Rosemary heard the witch's cracked voice: "A present—for my birthday."

She grabbed Freddy and smelled his fur. Just the same—milk, warmth, fire, long nights sleeping under warm, fusty covers. All the things Mathilda had never had—she had given back to Rosemary.